To Katie
from Grandma Hayes
Christmas 1991

The ANNE of GREEN GABLES TREASURY

VIKING

The ANNE of GREEN GABLES TREASURY

CAROLYN STROM COLLINS
CHRISTINA WYSS ERIKSSON

VIKING

VIKING

Published by the Penguin Group

Penguin Books Canada Ltd, 10 Alcorn Ave, Toronto, Ontario, Canada M4V 1E4

Penguin Books Ltd, 27 Wrights Lane, London W8 5TZ, England

Viking Penguin Inc., 375 Hudson Street, New York, New York 10014, USA

Penguin Books Australia Ltd, Ringwood, Victoria, Australia

Penguin Books (NZ) Ltd, 182 – 190 Wairau Road, Auckland 10, New Zealand

Penguin Books Ltd, Registered Offices: Harmondsworth, Middlesex, England

First published 1991

1 3 5 7 9 10 8 6 4 2

Printed and bound in Italy.

Canadian Cataloguing in Publication Data

Collins, Carolyn
      The Anne of Green Gables treasury
ISBN 0 – 670 – 82591 – 3

1. Montgomery, L. M. (Lucy Maud), 1874 – 1942. Anne of
Green Gables.   2. Handicraft.   3. Amusements.   4. Cookery.
I. Eriksson, Christina Wyss.   II. Montgomery, L. M. (Lucy Maud),
1874 – 1942. Anne of Green Gables.   III. Title.
PS8526.05A63   1989   793   C88 – 094773 – X
PZ7.M6Ann   1989

Dedicated to the memory of
L.M. Montgomery,
who bequeathed a love for beauty,
nobility of spirit,
and devotion to highest ideals
to her beloved character,
Anne of Green Gables.

CONTENTS

ACKNOWLEDGEMENTS

We acknowledge with much gratitude the gracious assistance of many people who shared with us their knowledge of the life and times of L.M. Montgomery and the history of Green Gables.

We are endlessly grateful to Barbara MacDonald of Parks Canada for making available to us the research for the restoration of Green Gables house in Prince Edward Island National Park, for allowing us to spend many hours reviewing documents and archival photographs, and for patiently answering our many questions about the details of the house and grounds.

We would also like to thank Shirley K. Wigmore, Special Collections Librarian, Jackson Library, Ontario Institute for Studies in Education, Toronto; Jill Shefrin, Osborne Collection of Early Children's Books, Toronto Public Library; Edward MacDonald and his staff at the Prince Edward Island Heritage Foundation; Marilyn Bell, Prince Edward Island Archives; George MacKay, Malpeque Gardens, Prince Edward Island; George Campbell, Anne of Green Gables Museum, Prince Edward Island; the staff of the L.M. Montgomery Birthplace Museum, New London, Prince Edward

Island; and the Prince Edward Island Department of Agriculture, Four-H Division. All gave us invaluable assistance in our search for information about nineteenth-century Prince Edward Island.

In Minnesota, we are grateful for the resources of the Minnesota Historical Society and the libraries of Hennepin County, Ramsey County, Minneapolis, St. Paul and General Mills, Inc.; the University of Minnesota Arboretum; and to Tom Wheeler of Hermes Floral for his contribution of quantities of rose petals for our seemingly endless experiments in making potpourri.

We owe much to our editors at Penguin Canada, Catherine Yolles, Iris Skeoch, Laurel Bernard, Shelley Tanaka and Mary Adachi; the designer, Gord Pronk, and Nelly Toomey of Pronk&Associates for their invaluable suggestions, assistance and expertise.

Many thanks go to our literary agent and friend, Jeanne Hanson, who has given much advice and support throughout the entire project.

Finally, to our dear families – Andy and Mark, Caroline and Drew, Aaron and Sarah Jane – who persevered through the years of our research, testing and writing about the world of Anne of Green Gables, we offer infinite gratitude for their patience, encouragement and enthusiasm.

— *Carolyn Strom Collins and Christina Wyss Eriksson*

Note on the Illustrations

The illustrations in the *Anne of Green Gables Treasury* reflect as accurately as possible the elements that would have made up Anne's world – Green Gables and its furnishings; the clothing Anne, Marilla and Diana would have worn; and the various items they would have used in their daily lives. All of these things actually existed and, thanks to photographs, articles, books and other archival material for reference, could be illustrated precisely as Anne would have known them.

Illustrating Anne herself, however, was much more challenging. Though almost real to many of her admirers, Anne is a fictitious character and the only true pictures of her are those we readers create for ourselves from the occasional descriptions of her in the Anne books. Her most striking feature, of course, is her hair, decidedly red, mellowing to a rich auburn as she grows into adulthood. Her facial features are "delicate" – a pointed chin, a nice nose (with seven freckles that appear if she does not wear her hat) and large grey-green expressive eyes. She is tall and slender, rather gangly as a child but graceful as an adult.

Her "portrait" has been painted by many artists and she has been portrayed on film and on the stage by a number of actresses. But it is surely impossible to reproduce those elusive qualities that created Anne's unique beauty, for, as Miss Josephine Barry stated, Anne had "as many shades as a rainbow and every shade is the prettiest while it lasts." Rather than add yet another version of Anne to the many existing ones, we requested that Anne's face not be shown in the illustrations for this book so that each reader may continue to envision Anne as she wishes in that magnificent realm of her own imagination.

—*C.S.C. and C.W.E.*

INTRODUCTION

Although both of us read and loved the Anne books as children, we became intrigued with them again when our daughters began to read them several years ago. We found ourselves enjoying these "children's books" even more as adults than we had as children! Perhaps because the plots were familiar to us, we could take more time to savour the rich descriptions of the setting and the bits of wisdom scattered throughout the funny, sad and exciting incidents in Anne's life.

Much of the charm of the Anne books lies in those details of everyday life in the Canadian Maritimes from the late 1800s through the end of World War I. As we talked about the books, we began to wonder if our children, growing up in a world of central heating and indoor plumbing, automobiles and shopping centres, television and computers, could possibly understand what Anne's world was really like. So, as mothers will, we took on the project of researching a bit of the background of the Anne books on their behalf.

We began by making lists of things that our daughters wanted to know more about and added to the lists as we read through the Anne books once again. What would Anne have had for meals? How was food prepared? Did Marilla have a refrigerator? These questions led us to find out more about how the household was run, and we discovered that there was a tremendous amount of work involved just in putting a meal on the table! Wood had to be chopped for the cookstove, water had to be drawn from the well and brought into the house, eggs had to be gathered, cows had to be milked and butter churned, and on and on. We were awed – and so were our daughters.

We wanted to know more about Anne's world. What was it like to go to school in a one-room schoolhouse, and what were those "Royal Readers" that Anne kept referring to? How were they different from the books in today's schools? Could eleven-year-old girls really do patchwork and crochet and knit? What did ladies' eardrops, scarlet lightning and Bouncing Bet look like? Could we grow some of them in our own gardens? What did Anne's dresses look like, and why did she have to lengthen her skirts and put up her hair when she turned seventeen?

Our list of questions grew longer and longer and, as we found answers, we began to think that other readers might also want to learn more about Anne's fascinating world. Eventually, we decided to compile the information into a book.

What we thought would be a few pleasant mornings spent in our branch library became a five-year obsession! We searched through cookbooks of the period for authentic recipes, we found copies of the Royal Readers and other textbooks that were in use during the time Anne would have been in school, and we taught ourselves to crochet lace and concoct potpourri just as Anne and her friends must have done. We even planted our gardens with as many of the flowers mentioned in the Anne books as we could manage!

Our quest for Anne's way of life took us to many more libraries, museums, historical societies, archives, special collections, antique stores and, eventually, to Prince Edward Island itself. We visited Green Gables, taking reams of notes and dozens of photographs, for we wanted our readers to have as authentic a picture as possible of the house. We were pleased to discover that Green Gables had been restored in 1986 to more accurately depict the house as described in the Anne books. Photographs taken by L.M. Montgomery of that house and others in the area also helped Parks Canada curators select wallpaper, carpets, curtains, furniture and accessories for Green Gables, so that today's visitors can experience the house as Anne, Marilla and Matthew must have known it.

As it happened, our own interest coincided with a general renewal of interest in Anne and her creator, L.M. Montgomery. A much-acclaimed television series based on *Anne of Green Gables* was shown in 1985; a sequel followed in 1987. And L.M. Montgomery's own journals were published in two volumes – the first in 1985, the second in 1987 – enhancing several biographies and collections of her letters and articles that had already been published.

We hope that the results of our explorations, much of which is revealed in this companion to the Anne books, will entice readers to create for themselves a bit of the world of *Anne of Green Gables*.

The ANNE of GREEN GABLES TREASURY

Lucy Maud Montgomery
30 November 1874 — 24 April 1942

CHAPTER 1

L. M. Montgomery
and the Anne Books

"Nothing I have ever written gave me so much pleasure to write. I made my 'Anne' a real human girl."

(SELECTED JOURNALS OF LUCY MAUD MONTGOMERY, AUGUST 16, 1907)

Lucy Maud Montgomery was born on November 30, 1874, in a small house in the town of Clifton on Prince Edward Island, Canada. She was the only child of Clara Macneill Woolner Montgomery and Hugh John Montgomery. Their house in Clifton is now a museum where visitors can see, among other things, the room in which Maud was born, many of her scrapbooks, and her wedding dress.

When Maud (as she liked to be called) was only twenty-one months old, her mother died of tuberculosis, and Maud was taken to live with her grandparents, Alexander and Lucy Woolner Macneill, who lived about twelve miles away near the little town of Cavendish. Maud's father continued to run his store in Clifton while he pursued other business on the Island and, eventually, in western Canada. Maud adored her father, but since he lived in Clifton and travelled a great deal, her visits with him were occasional and brief.

When Maud was seven, her father left for Prince Albert, Saskatchewan (about 2,500 miles from Cavendish), where he eventually settled and remarried. At the age of sixteen, Maud travelled to Prince Albert to live with her father and his new wife and baby. Although she was homesick for Cavendish, she was happy to be with her father at last: "It is lovely to be with father again…" she wrote in her journal. "He is *such* a darling. His eyes just *shine* with love when he looks at me."

After a year in Prince Albert, however, Maud reluctantly decided that she should return to her grandparents on Prince Edward Island. Her stepmother, apparently, was making her life miserable:

I shall be sorry to leave father…but…It will be so wonderful to escape from the atmosphere of suspicion and petty malice and persecution which Mrs. Montgomery seems to exhale wherever she is. Sometimes I feel as if I were literally smothering in it. I work my fingers to the bone for her and her children and I am not even civilly treated for it….

Maud returned to Cavendish in September, 1891. She wrote to her father often and continued to feel very close to him until he died in 1900, when Maud was twenty-five.

Living with her grandparents was not easy, either, because they were quite elderly and very strict. They lived a quiet life, farming and keeping the Cavendish post office, and Maud often felt lonely. Her lively personality did not match their seriousness, so there was little joy in her life except that which she created for herself through her writing; from the time she was a young girl she kept a journal and wrote poems and stories.

Like Anne, Maud received her first-class teacher's licence after one year instead of the usual two, and she spent a year teaching on the Island before going to university in Nova Scotia. When she had completed her studies, she returned to Prince Edward Island to teach. Her grandfather's death in 1898 brought an end to Maud's teaching career; she felt her place was back in Cavendish with her grandmother. Except for a brief period when she worked for the

Halifax newspapers, she stayed on the Cavendish farm until her grandmother died.

During these years, Maud continued to write. A good number of her poems and stories were published in newspapers and magazines, and in the spring of 1905, she began to work on her first novel, *Anne of Green Gables*. When she finished the manuscript about a year and a half later, she sent it to several publishers, but none of them wanted to publish it. Discouraged, she put the novel away in a hat box and forgot it. A year or so later she came upon the manuscript while rummaging through the closet. This time she decided to send it to the L. C. Page Company of Boston. They promptly accepted it, and when the book was published in June, 1908, Maud was elated:

My book came to-day, fresh from the publishers. I candidly confess that it was for me a proud, wonderful, thrilling moment! There in my hand lay the material realization of all the dreams and hopes and ambitions and struggles of my whole conscious existence – my first book! Not a great book at all – but mine, mine, mine, – something to which I had given birth – something which, but for me, would never have existed…

Maud always insisted that the Anne books were not auto-biographical, but there are certainly many similarities in Anne's and Maud's stories. Anne and Maud were both orphans who were brought up by strict, no-nonsense guardians in farming communities on the north shore of Prince Edward Island. Many of Maud's favourite places in Cavendish became Anne's in Avonlea – Green Gables itself, Lover's Lane, the Haunted Wood, the brook and the old log bridge, the little schoolhouse with its spruce grove, and many others. Maud also gave Anne her own intense love of beauty and nature, a passion for reading and learning and excelling, and a vivid imagination, from which sprang an infinite supply of imaginary friends and stories (the Katie Maurice who lived behind one of the glass doors in a china cupboard was Maud's imaginary friend before she was Anne's).

During the time she was caring for her grandmother and writing *Anne of Green Gables* and the sequel, *Anne of Avonlea*, Maud became engaged to Ewan Macdonald, the minister of the Cavendish Presbyterian Church. She finally agreed to marry Ewan only if he would wait until her grandmother no longer needed her. They were engaged for five years, marrying a few months after her grandmother died in 1911.

The Macdonalds moved to the small town of Leaskdale, Ontario, where Ewan was a minister for the next fifteen years. They had two sons, Chester and Stuart. Writing continued to be an important part of Maud's life, and it provided a kind of escape from the demanding life of being a mother and minister's wife. In addition to the Anne books, she published fifteen other books and a number of stories, poems and articles. She continued to keep her journal and wrote to her friends frequently. She also answered her own fan mail, which she received in large amounts.

In 1926 the Macdonalds moved to Norval, Ontario. Ewan retired in 1936, and he and Maud moved to Toronto to live out their remaining years.

Maud always thought of Prince Edward Island as her true home, though she never lived there again after her marriage. She visited the Island often and, when she died on April 24, 1942, her family took her to Cavendish to be buried in the cemetery close to her beloved Green Gables.

Anne's Prince Edward Island ▶

Prince Edward Island

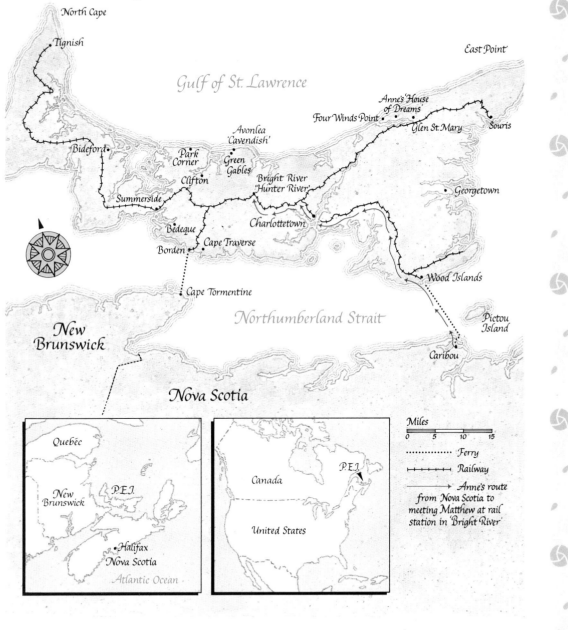

North Cape

Tignish

Gulf of St. Lawrence

East Point

Anne's House of Dreams

Four Winds Point

Glen St. Mary

Souris

Bideford

Avonlea 'Cavendish'

Park Corner

Green Gables

Clifton

Bright River 'Hunter River'

Georgetown

Summerside

Charlottetown

Bedeque

Cape Traverse

Borden

Wood Islands

Cape Tormentine

Northumberland Strait

Pictou Island

New Brunswick

Caribou

Nova Scotia

Quebec

New Brunswick

P.E.I.

Halifax
Nova Scotia

Atlantic Ocean

Canada

P.E.I.

United States

Miles
0   5   10   15

·········· Ferry

+++++++ Railway

——→ Anne's route from Nova Scotia to meeting Matthew at rail station in 'Bright River'

The Anne Books

Little did L. M. Montgomery realize that *Anne of Green Gables* would prove so popular with readers that seven *more* books about Anne would eventually be published. When the first Anne book was such a success, Maud's publisher requested a sequel, so she began work on *Anne of Avonlea* which was published in 1909. In all, she wrote eight Anne books over about thirty years. Although the books chronicle Anne's life from age eleven through middle age, they were not written in chronological order. *Anne of Windy Poplars* and *Anne of Ingleside* were not written and published until the 1930s, after *Rainbow Valley* and *Rilla of Ingleside*.

ANNE OF GREEN GABLES (1908)

Matthew and Marilla Cuthbert, an elderly brother and sister who live at Green Gables Farm on Prince Edward Island, have applied to a Nova Scotia orphanage for a boy to live with them and help them run their farm. Due to a misunderstanding, however, they are sent an eleven-year-old girl instead. After much deliberation, they decide to keep the imaginative, vivacious and temperamental Anne Shirley, and life at Green Gables is never the same again.

Before her first year at Green Gables is over, Anne has managed to insult Marilla's friend, Mrs. Rachel Lynde; scandalize the Sunday-morning crowd at church with her outlandish hat decoration; crack her slate over the head of the handsomest boy in school; and mistakenly intoxicate her best friend with Marilla's homemade currant wine.

These are only the beginning of Anne's "adventures" growing up at Green Gables. Her romantic notions cause her some harrowing moments in The Haunted Wood across the brook and, later, in the Lake of Shining Waters while dramatizing Tennyson's story of "the unfortunate lily maid." In her desperation to rid herself of her "lifelong sorrow" (her emphatically red hair), she also buys a bottle of dye from a peddlar. Her visions of dramatic black-as-a-raven tresses turn to horror when her hair emerges from its treatment a ghastly shade of green.

Fortunately, Anne copes with her propensity for mistakes by learning from each one and comforts herself, and Marilla, with the thought that: "There *must* be a limit to the mistakes one person can make, and when I get to the end of them, then I'll be through with them."

Though Anne stumbles often through her first few years at Green Gables, her many mistakes are balanced by her cheerful disposition and her determination to succeed. Anne grows into a confident, lovely young woman with many hopes and ambitions.

ANNE OF AVONLEA (1909)

At age sixteen, Anne becomes the teacher at her childhood school near Green Gables and finds that teaching is more difficult than she had ever dreamed. And even though she is a "fullfledged schoolma'am," her adventures outside the classroom continue. Who else but Anne of Green Gables would fall through the roof of a chicken coop while searching for a china platter in a thundershower? And who else but Anne would prepare an elaborate luncheon for a famous visitor, only to have the guest of honour fail to arrive until several days later when Anne is spring-cleaning?

Six-year-old twins Davy and Dora Keith come to live at Green Gables and provide plenty of challenges for Anne and Marilla along the way, from falling into fresh lemon meringue pies while climbing the pantry shelves, to splashing through mud puddles on the way to Sunday School.

Anne and Diana continue their friendship and their explorations in the fields and forests around Avonlea, discovering a hidden garden with a romantic history and a secluded stone cottage, whose occupant, Miss Lavendar Lewis, entertains pretend guests at tea!

A hint of romance replaces the old rivalry between Anne and Gilbert Blythe, and Anne begins to wonder if "romance did not come into one's life with pomp and blare," but "crept to one's side like an old friend through quiet ways." With these thoughts, Anne reluctantly steps from girlhood into young womanhood, "with all its charm and mystery, its pain and gladness."

ANNE OF THE ISLAND (1915)

After teaching for two years at Avonlea School, Anne continues her education at Redmond College in Nova Scotia. Gilbert Blythe and Charlie Sloane from Avonlea are there at the same time, as well as Anne's good friends Priscilla Grant and Stella Maynard. The girls rent a charming little cottage called Patty's Place, and set up housekeeping there. Anne's Prince Charming then enters her life in the form of Roy Gardner.

Over the next two years, Anne almost convinces herself that she is in love with Roy, but when he finally asks her to marry him, she suddenly realizes that in spite of his "good looks and knack of paying romantic compliments," he does not "belong" in her life.

Anne begins to give up hope that she will ever find her romantic ideal. Not until she learns that Gilbert Blythe is gravely ill with typhoid fever does she fully understand how much she cares for him. She spends many agonizing hours fearing that Gilbert will die, never knowing that she loved him. However, Gilbert recovers and, on a late-summer afternoon walk to Hester Gray's garden, receives Anne's rapturous acceptance of his proposal.

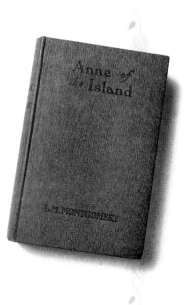

ANNE OF WINDY POPLARS (1936)

While Gilbert is away at medical school, Anne accepts the principalship at the high school at Summerside, about thirty miles from Green Gables. Boarding at Windy Poplars with two elderly widows and their housekeeper, Rebecca Dew, Anne proceeds to win the hearts of the townspeople (including the difficult Pringle clan), and spends three very happy years there. She rescues little Elizabeth Grayson, who lives next door with her strict grandmother, from a life of discouragement and despair, and even manages to transform one of her fellow teachers, the embittered Katherine Brooke, into a happy "kindred spirit."

ANNE'S HOUSE OF DREAMS (1922)

Anne and Gilbert are married in the old apple orchard at Green Gables and spend their first two years of married life in the little "House of Dreams" on the shore of Four Winds Harbour, about sixty miles from Avonlea. There they become fast friends with Captain Jim, keeper of the Four Winds lighthouse; Miss Cornelia Bryant, an opinionated but kindhearted spinster; and Leslie Moore, a beautiful young woman with a tragic past, whose life is changed forever because of her friendship with Anne and Gilbert.

ANNE OF INGLESIDE (1939)

With their young family outgrowing the little House of Dreams, Anne reluctantly agrees to move to the nearby village of Glen St. Mary. Ingleside is a large house "old enough to have dignity and repose and traditions, and new enough to be comfortable and up-to-date." There are twelve acres of trees, a walled garden, an orchard, and even a brook and pond nearby – an ideal setting in which to bring up six active children.

"Baby" Jem, born in the House of Dreams, is now seven years old, and five more children have been born to Anne and Gilbert – Walter, twins Nan and Di, Shirley and Rilla. Each seems to have inherited a bit of Anne's talent for adventure, and they become known to some in Glen St. Mary as "that pack of Ingleside demons." But Anne understands that their liveliness, curiosity and exuberance are just a natural part of growing up!

RAINBOW VALLEY (1919)

There is a new minister in town, and his four children join forces with the Blythe children to create plenty of merry mayhem in Glen St. Mary. Ghosts in a neighbour's garden, "concerts" in the graveyard, a pet rooster that comes to Sunday dinner, and several nearly disastrous matchmaking schemes keep life in the little harbour town lively.

RILLA OF INGLESIDE (1921)

Instead of the round of parties and dances she had envisioned, fifteen-year-old Rilla, Anne's youngest daughter, grows up in the dark shadow of World War I. She watches her three brothers leave home for the war and anxiously waits with Anne and Gilbert for word from them.

Ingleside becomes a centre of activity for Red Cross work, and Rilla finds herself rolling bandages and hemming sheets for the first time in her life. Anne's advice that "we will all have to do a great many things in the months ahead of us that we have never done before" proves prophetic, but even she could not have guessed that one of Rilla's war-time contributions would be "adopting" a newborn baby whose mother has died and whose father is at the front!

(Overleaf) The Village of Avonlea

Carmody
Road

Echo Lodge

Avonlea

1. Green Gables
2. Diana's House ("Orchard Slope")
3. Mrs. Lynde's House
4. Presbyterian Church
5. The Manse
6. The Post Office
7. Avonlea School
8. Lover's Lane
9. Avonlea Hall
10. Gilbert's House
11. Lake of Shining Waters

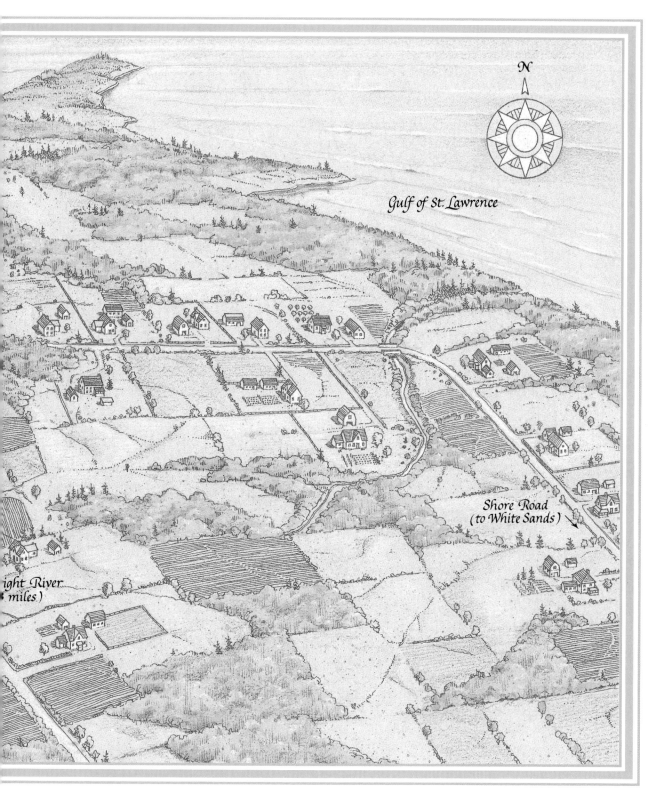

Gulf of St. Lawrence

Shore Road
(to White Sands)

ight River
miles)

Anne's Family Tree

Since Anne was orphaned as a baby, the details of her family history are few. But we know that she was born in Bolingbroke, Nova Scotia, in March, 1866, and that she was the first and only child of Walter and Bertha Shirley. Both parents died of fever when Anne was only three months old.

Working from the dates in *Rilla of Ingleside* and from clues in the other Anne books, we have been able to calculate Anne's and Gilbert's years of birth as well as those of their children. Anne's parents' birth dates are approximate, based on the statement Anne made when she was twenty years old: "Just to think of it – mother was younger than I am now when I was born."

Since Matthew and Marilla were not related to Anne, they do not belong in her "official" family tree. However, we do know that Matthew was sixty when Anne came to Green Gables, and that he died when she was sixteen, so his dates can be determined as 1817 to 1882. Marilla was born in 1822 and died sometime between 1907 and 1914, when she would have been close to ninety.

Anne's Family ▶

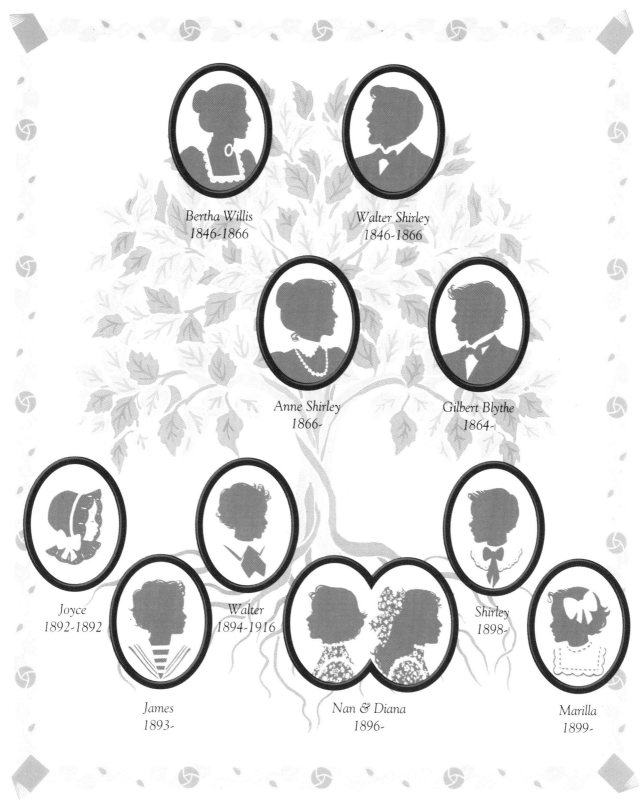

Bertha Willis
1846-1866

Walter Shirley
1846-1866

Anne Shirley
1866-

Gilbert Blythe
1864-

Joyce
1892-1892

Walter
1894-1916

Shirley
1898-

James
1893-

Nan & Diana
1896-

Marilla
1899-

CHAPTER 2

Anne's World

"This Island is the bloomiest place. I just love it already, and I'm so glad I'm going to live here. I've always heard that Prince Edward Island was the prettiest place in the world…" (ANNE OF GREEN GABLES, II)

Anne Shirley was just eleven years old when she first came to Prince Edward Island, but she never changed her mind about it being the "prettiest place in the world," even after she had grown up and visited other places.

Prince Edward Island is nestled just beyond the curved shores of Nova Scotia and New Brunswick in the Gulf of St. Lawrence. The Micmac Indians who first settled the Island about two thousand years ago called it "Abegweit," which means "a land cradled upon the waves." Jacques Cartier, the great French explorer, discovered it in 1534 and called it "the fairest land 'tis possible to see." Cartier named it Ile St-Jean, and when the British won the Island from France in 1758, they called it Island of St. John. Not until 1799 did it finally become Prince Edward Island, named for the father of Queen Victoria.

Prince Edward Island is Canada's birthplace, for it was in its capital, Charlottetown, that the Confederation of Canada was first discussed in 1864. It also holds the distinction of being Canada's smallest province, for it is only 140 miles long and 40 miles across at its widest point.

One of Anne's first questions to Matthew was "what *does* make the roads red?" Of course, the roads then weren't paved, so Anne was noticing the Island's natural blood-red soil, so rich in iron that it oxidizes or rusts when exposed to the air. It is very good farm land, and most of the province is still given to farming, just as it was in Anne's day. The Island is famous for its potatoes, as it was when Matthew was growing them in the 1800s. Other major industries are fishing (and canning the fish, lobster, oysters and clams) and tourism. Thousands of visitors come to the Island every year to enjoy its natural beauty and to see the little farm that L.M. Montgomery made famous.

Green Gables

"It's lovely to be going home and know it's home…I love Green Gables already, and I never loved any place before. No place ever seemed like home." (ANNE OF GREEN GABLES, X)

Although Anne Shirley is a fictional character, Green Gables is a real place. It is situated on a small piece of farmland on the north shore of Prince Edward Island, near the village of Cavendish ("Avonlea" in the Anne books).

When L.M. Montgomery began to write *Anne of Green Gables*, she used the farmhouse that belonged to her cousins, David and Margaret Macneill, as the setting. Like Matthew and Marilla Cuthbert, the Macneills were an elderly brother and sister who ran the family farm. The house was just a few hundred yards away from the house that Maud lived in with her grandparents, so Maud visited her cousins often. She especially enjoyed walking in Lover's Lane.

Since 1936, Parks Canada has maintained the Macneill home (now known as Green Gables) and the surrounding acreage as Prince Edward Island National Park and, during most of the year, the house is open to visitors. Green Gables today has clapboard siding painted white with dark-green trim and shutters, but during the years Anne would have lived there (1877-1884), the house was shingled. Since there was a sawmill in Cavendish in the mid-1850s, buildings could be made of shingles or clapboards rather than logs or stones (as they had been in the early years of settling the Island).

The house stands on a hill that slopes down to a little creek; across the creek are woods full of birch, maple and spruce trees. The Haunted Wood is up the hill beyond these woods and does, indeed,

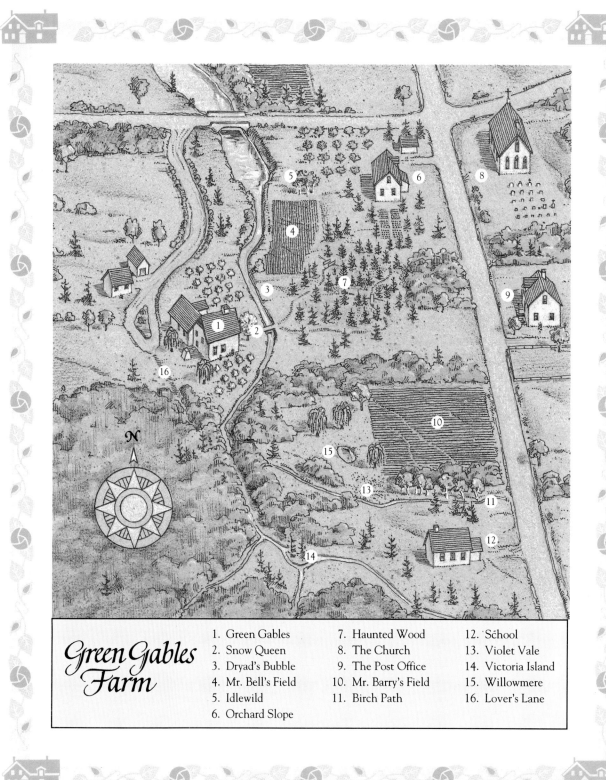

Green Gables Farm

1. Green Gables
2. Snow Queen
3. Dryad's Bubble
4. Mr. Bell's Field
5. Idlewild
6. Orchard Slope

7. Haunted Wood
8. The Church
9. The Post Office
10. Mr. Barry's Field
11. Birch Path

12. School
13. Violet Vale
14. Victoria Island
15. Willowmere
16. Lover's Lane

give the startling impression of being haunted, with its ghostly-looking pine trees. There is also a small meadow (Mr. Bell's field) near the Haunted Wood. Lover's Lane winds through more woods to the southwest of the house. Walking through these woods today, it is easy to imagine Anne and Diana strolling to and from school or racing back and forth between Green Gables and Orchard Slope.

The front door of Green Gables opens into a tiny vestibule; another door opens into the front hallway (two doors helped to keep blasts of cold winter air from entering the house). To the right of the entry is a steep flight of stairs leading to the second floor. To the left is the parlour, which was closed off most of the time so that it would stay clean and neat for special occasions.

The sitting room is actually a combined sitting room/dining room, with a dining table and chairs and buffet on one side for company meals or Sunday dinners. On the other side of the room are comfortable chairs, a large round table, a bookcase/desk and a small heating stove. After the kitchen, this was the room the family used the most.

Between the sitting room and kitchen is a small bedroom where Matthew would have slept. This room is simply furnished with a narrow bed, a washstand and a trunk. The trunk was used as a bedside table, as well as for storing clothing.

The centre of activity at Green Gables was the kitchen. It was used for cooking and serving everyday family meals, and as a sitting room:

The kitchen at Green Gables was a cheerful apartment – or would have been cheerful if it had not been so painfully clean as to give it something of the appearance of an unused parlour....Here sat Marilla Cuthbert, when she sat at all...knitting, and the table behind her was laid for supper. (ANNE OF GREEN GABLES, 1)

The heart of the kitchen was the large black iron cookstove. The introduction of the cookstove in the mid-nineteenth century placed cooking a step above the open-fire cooking of the early settlers, opening up a whole new world of culinary possibilities. The stove was much more efficient and more reliable than a fireplace, so a greater variety of food could be prepared. It was not only used for cooking, but for heating the large room. This was comforting in the harsh cold of winter, but extremely uncomfortable in the summer. Fortunately, Prince Edward Island summers are mild, and since the main meal of the day was served at noon, much of the heat of the stove would leave the house during the afternoon.

Green Gables was not equipped with running water in Anne's day; water had to be drawn from the well near the back door for cooking, dishwashing, household chores, laundering clothes and bathing. The well at Green Gables "was the deepest in Avonlea," which meant there was an ample water supply, though this was cold comfort when Anne had to search there for a missing Dora Keith.

The storage of food commanded much space in farm homes. Staples such as flour and sugar, as well as prepared foods, canned goods and dishes, were stored in a room called a pantry. Anne's Green Gables had two pantries — a "sitting-room pantry" and a "kitchen pantry." The walls of each would have been lined with shelves, and there may also have been some cabinets and a work table.

Some foods, such as apples, carrots, onions and potatoes, were stored in large bins in the cellar. Fruits and vegetables too perishable to store in the cellar for any length of time were canned or dried in the summer to last until the next canning season (the Mason jar had been available since the 1850s for home canning). Meats were smoked, cured in brine or dried in the fall to supplement fresh meat through the winter.

A constant challenge was keeping insects and rodents out of the house, as Anne learned when she discovered a drowned mouse in a pitcher of pudding sauce that she had neglected to cover! Of course, there was no plastic wrap or foil in those days; instead, saucers, plates, inverted bowls or clean kitchen cloths would be used to cover food.

Although not mentioned in any of the Anne books, it is

possible that Marilla's kitchen was furnished with an icebox. A small compartment for food would be topped by a compartment for a large block of ice. The cold air created by the ice would drift down into the food compartment. However, with eggs and milk available fresh each day from the hens and cows on the farm, refrigeration was not as necessary as it is today. (Are you wondering where the blocks of ice for the icebox would have come from? In those days, ice was cut from the frozen ponds in winter and stored in ice-houses for use in the warmer months. The blocks of ice would be surrounded by thick layers of hay or sawdust to keep them from melting, even in summer.)

Originally, the kitchen wing of Green Gables did not have a second storey as it does today. However, above the parlour/sitting-room wing was a second storey containing four rooms – Anne's bedroom and the spare room on the front of the house; Marilla's bedroom and one other room at the rear.

Anne's room was the east gable room – the room beneath the part of the house that comes together in a point. It is just over the front entrance. When Anne first arrived at Green Gables, the little room was sparsely furnished and very plainly decorated:

The whitewashed walls were so painfully bare and staring that she thought they must ache over their own bareness. The floor was bare, too, except for a round braided mat in the middle such as Anne had never seen before. In one corner was the bed, a high, old-fashioned one, with four dark, low-turned posts. In the other corner was the aforesaid three-cornered table adorned with a fat, red velvet pincushion hard enough to turn the point of the most adventurous pin. Above it hung a little six by eight mirror. Midway between the table and bed was the window, with an icy white muslin frill over it, and opposite it was the washstand. The whole apartment was of a rigidity not to be described in words, but which sent a shiver to the very marrow of Anne's bones. (ANNE OF GREEN GABLES, III)

After Anne had lived in it for a while, however, the room took on a great deal of personality. By the time she was sixteen, her little room was transformed:

The east gable was a very different place from what it had been on that night four years before, when Anne had felt its bareness penetrate to the marrow of her spirit with its inhospitable chill. Changes had crept in, Marilla conniving at them resignedly, until it was as sweet and dainty a nest as a young girl could desire....The floor was covered with a pretty matting, and the curtains that softened the high window and fluttered in the vagrant breezes were of pale green art muslin. The walls, hung not with gold and silver brocade tapestry, but with a dainty apple blossom paper, were adorned with a few good pictures given Anne by Mrs. Allan....There was no "mahogany furniture," but there was a white-painted bookcase filled with books, a cushioned wicker rocker, a toilet table befrilled with white muslin, a quaint, gilt-framed mirror with chubby pink cupids and purple grapes painted over its arched top, that used to hang in the spare room, and a low white bed. (ANNE OF GREEN GABLES, XXXIII)

If you visit Green Gables today, you will find Anne's room decorated in precisely this way.

The spare room was the bedroom reserved for guests. Anne was in awe of spare rooms, perhaps because they were denied her in her early childhood when she was a servant in other households. Even Marilla would not permit the "stray waif" (as she thought of Anne that first night at Green Gables) to sleep in the spare room. Though the furnishings were not elaborate, they were of the best quality the Cuthberts could afford. Linens were trimmed in lace, and the walls were papered. Like most bedrooms in houses of the era, it contained a washstand with a large china pitcher and bowl. These were used for the daily sponge baths common at that time. (Tub bathing was rare. Some households had a ritual of Saturday night bathing with water heated on the kitchen stove and a tin tub set on the kitchen floor. L.M. Montgomery remarks in her journal that her grandmother was not in favour of tub bathing, but Maud insisted on a bath at least every two weeks!)

Marilla's bedroom was at the back corner of the house, over the dining/sitting room. It was rarely visited by Anne and apparently was used only for sleeping and dressing by Marilla.

Closets were not common in houses at that time. Instead, clothes were stored in trunks and large cupboards called wardrobes. Out-of-season clothing was kept in the attic with plenty of mothballs or moth-deterring herbs. Anne's bedroom is the only one at Green Gables with a closet, perhaps because the space was created naturally above the stairwell.

In the present Green Gables, the fourth upstairs room (the west gable room) is furnished as a sewing room with a treadle sewing machine, quilting frame, spinning wheel, yarn winder, trunk and other sewing accessories. The west window provides good light, so the room may well have been used this way, especially since sewing was an almost constant activity in homes like Green Gables. The room could also have been used for storage. When Davy and Dora Keith came to live at Green Gables, Davy slept in the west gable room. (The upstairs rooms would not have been heated, so the family would not have spent much time in them during the winter months.)

In 1914, many years after Anne would have left Green Gables, a second storey was added over the kitchen. Today, one of the rooms in this addition has been furnished as a bedroom for a hired man, and a small area is used for storing some items that were probably used during the Anne years – snowshoes, trunks and tools. The other rooms are used as office space for the staff in charge of the house and are not open to the public.

Visiting Green Gables today is a moving experience for readers of *Anne of Green Gables*, for the house is furnished as closely as possible to the descriptions in the Anne books. One almost expects to see Anne herself dashing into the kitchen to tell Marilla about her latest adventure!

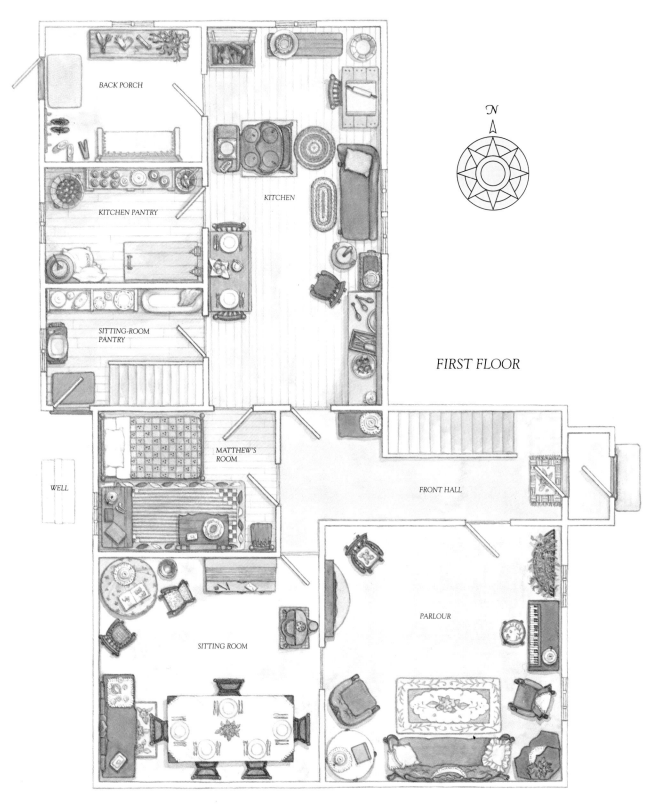

BACK PORCH

KITCHEN PANTRY

SITTING-ROOM
PANTRY

KITCHEN

N

FIRST FLOOR

WELL

MATTHEW'S
ROOM

FRONT HALL

SITTING ROOM

PARLOUR

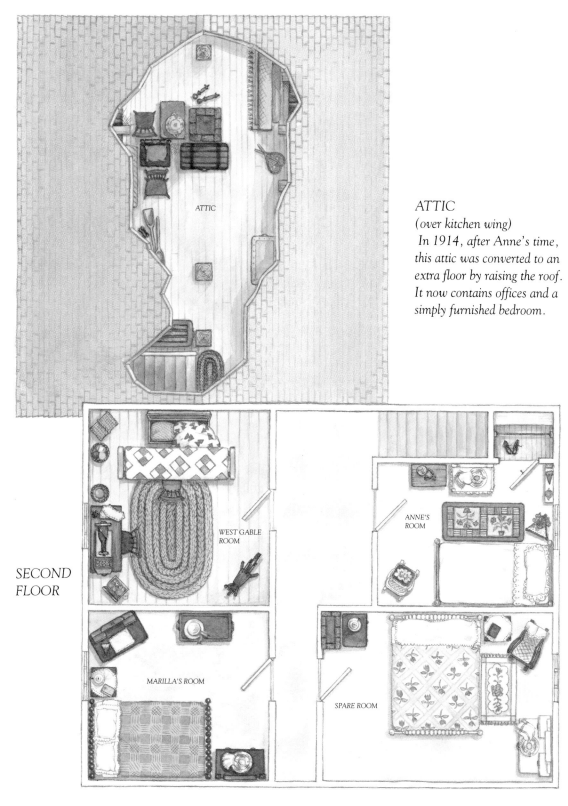

ATTIC

ATTIC
(over kitchen wing)
In 1914, after Anne's time,
this attic was converted to an
extra floor by raising the roof.
It now contains offices and a
simply furnished bedroom.

SECOND
FLOOR

WEST GABLE
ROOM

ANNE'S
ROOM

MARILLA'S ROOM

SPARE ROOM

CHAPTER 3

Through the Years

"Changes come all the time."　　　　　　　　　　(ANNE'S HOUSE OF DREAMS, XXXX)

The period in which Anne's story is set was an exciting one. The Civil War in the United States ended just the year before she was born. During Anne's girlhood, the Canadian provinces became united as the Dominion of Canada, and important new inventions such as the telephone, the automobile and the airplane were commanding attention. Mark Twain, Louisa May Alcott and Lewis Carroll were publishing their classic stories, and Queen Victoria celebrated her Gold and Diamond jubilees. The first candy bar, the teddy bear and chewing gum were introduced.

There were many other important events and innovations taking place from the time Anne was born (1866) until she was fifty-three years old – the period that the eight Anne books cover. We chose to include significant world events, births and deaths of some of the authors Anne admired, and inventions that made a difference to her life. Perhaps you can compare important dates in your own family history to those in this timetable and discover what was happening in the lives of your grandparents during those Anne years.

1866

Anne is born in March in Bolingbroke, Nova Scotia; both parents die of fever when she is three months old; Anne lives with Mr. and Mrs. Thomas in Marysville until she is eight

- First meeting of the Canadian legislature
- Dynamite is invented by Alfred Nobel
- Beatrix Potter, artist and author of *Peter Rabbit*, is born

1867

Anne is one year old

- The Dominion of Canada is formed
- Sir John A. Macdonald becomes the first prime minister of Canada
- Alaska is bought from Russia by the United States
- Marie Curie, discoverer of radium, is born
- Laura Ingalls Wilder, author of *Little House on the Prairie*, is born
- Barbed wire is patented in the United States

1868

Anne is two years old

- William E. Gladstone becomes prime minister of Great Britain
- Louisa May Alcott's *Little Women* is published

Sir John A. Macdonald

1869

Anne is three years old

- John W. Hyatt discovers celluloid, the forerunner of modern plastics
- Mahatma Gandhi is born

1870

Anne is four years old

- Charles Dickens, British author, dies
- Rosa Hartwick Thorpe publishes her poem, "Curfew Must Not Ring Tonight," recited by Prissy Andrews in the February, 1878, Avonlea concert

Mahatma Gandhi

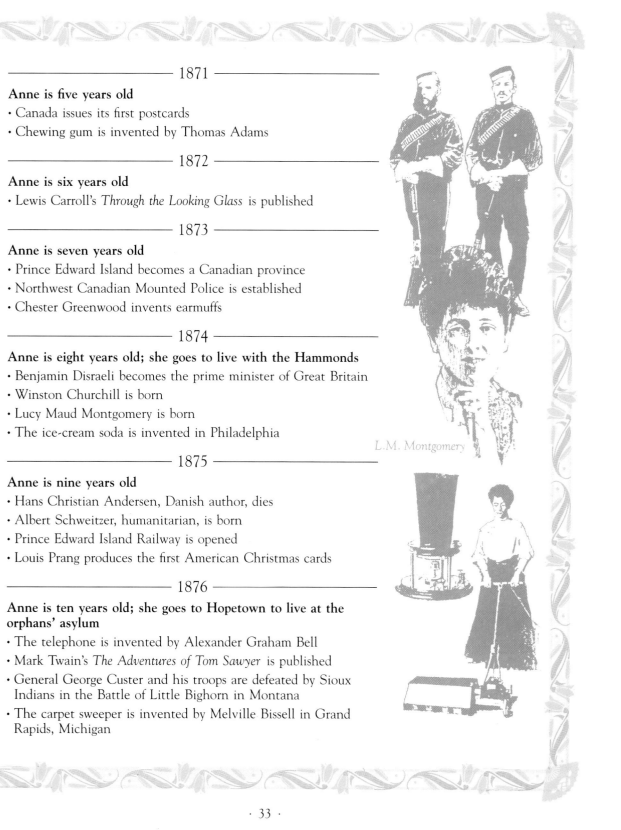

———————————— 1871 ————————————

Anne is five years old
• Canada issues its first postcards
• Chewing gum is invented by Thomas Adams

———————————— 1872 ————————————

Anne is six years old
• Lewis Carroll's *Through the Looking Glass* is published

———————————— 1873 ————————————

Anne is seven years old
• Prince Edward Island becomes a Canadian province
• Northwest Canadian Mounted Police is established
• Chester Greenwood invents earmuffs

———————————— 1874 ————————————

Anne is eight years old; she goes to live with the Hammonds
• Benjamin Disraeli becomes the prime minister of Great Britain
• Winston Churchill is born
• Lucy Maud Montgomery is born
• The ice-cream soda is invented in Philadelphia

L.M. Montgomery

———————————— 1875 ————————————

Anne is nine years old
• Hans Christian Andersen, Danish author, dies
• Albert Schweitzer, humanitarian, is born
• Prince Edward Island Railway is opened
• Louis Prang produces the first American Christmas cards

———————————— 1876 ————————————

Anne is ten years old; she goes to Hopetown to live at the orphans' asylum
• The telephone is invented by Alexander Graham Bell
• Mark Twain's *The Adventures of Tom Sawyer* is published
• General George Custer and his troops are defeated by Sioux Indians in the Battle of Little Bighorn in Montana
• The carpet sweeper is invented by Melville Bissell in Grand Rapids, Michigan

Albert Einstein

——————————— 1877 ———————————

Anne is eleven years old; she goes to Green Gables in June
- The phonograph is invented by Thomas A. Edison
- Anna Sewell's *Black Beauty* is published
- Euphemia Allen, age sixteen, publishes the first written version of "Chopsticks" in Britain

——————————— 1878 ———————————

Anne is twelve years old; she bakes "liniment cake" and breaks her ankle in a fall from the Barrys' kitchen roof; Matthew gives Anne the dress with puffed sleeves
- Gilbert and Sullivan's *H.M.S. Pinafore* is produced
- David Hughes invents the microphone

——————————— 1879 ———————————

Anne is thirteen years old; she dyes her hair green; she is rescued from the river by Gilbert; she begins studying for Queen's
- Albert Einstein, physicist, is born
- Prince of Wales College in Charlottetown is opened to women
- Ivory soap is introduced
- The first Charlottetown Festival is held

——————————— 1880 ———————————

Anne is fourteen years old
- William E. Gladstone becomes the prime minister of Great Britain
- Lew Wallace's *Ben Hur* is published (Anne must have had an advance copy – she was caught reading this in class in 1879!)
- Author Helen Keller is born
- Johanna Spyri's *Heidi* is published
- Edison invents the electric lightbulb
- Canned goods become available in stores
- The first baseball card is introduced
- Ned Kelly, Australian outlaw and folk hero, is hanged in Melbourne

1881

Anne is fifteen years old; she takes the entrance examination for Queen's; she recites "The Maiden's Vow" at the hotel concert; she enrols at Queen's College

- Clara Barton starts the American Red Cross
- Thomas Nast draws the modern version of Santa Claus

1882

Anne is sixteen years old; she earns her teacher's certificate and wins the Avery scholarship to Redmond College; Matthew dies; Anne begins teaching in Avonlea School; Davy and Dora Keith come to live at Green Gables

- Franklin D. Roosevelt is born
- Charles Darwin, author of *Origin of Species*, dies

1883

Anne is seventeen years old; she discovers Hester Gray's garden; Anne and Diana meet Miss Lavendar Lewis of Echo Lodge

- Robert Louis Stevenson's *Treasure Island* is published
- Carlo Collodi's *The Adventures of Pinocchio* is published in Italy
- Charles Stilwell invents the brown paper grocery bag

Franklin D. Roosevelt

1884

Anne is eighteen years old; Mrs. Rachel Lynde comes to live at Green Gables; Miss Lavendar Lewis is married to Stephen Irving; Anne enrols at Redmond College

- Women are allowed to vote in Canada for the first time
- Lewis Waterman invents the first practical fountain pen
- Mark Twain's *Huckleberry Finn* is published
- The first American roller-coaster is built in Coney Island, New York

——————————— 1885 ———————————

Anne is nineteen years old; Anne, Priscilla, Stella and Philippa move into Patty's Place

· Electric lights are introduced in Charlottetown, P.E.I.

· The Canadian Pacific transcontinental railway is completed

· The first commercially successful bicycle is introduced in the United States

——————————— 1886 ———————————

Anne is twenty years old; Gilbert proposes and is refused; Anne meets Roy Gardner

· Robert Louis Stevenson's *Dr. Jekyll and Mr. Hyde* is published

· The Statue of Liberty is dedicated

· Frances Hodgson Burnett's *Little Lord Fauntleroy* is published

· John S. Pemberton creates Coca-Cola

· C.M. Hall invents aluminium cookware

· Josephine Cochrane invents the first mechanical dishwasher

——————————— 1887 ———————————

Anne is twenty-one years old; Diana is married; Anne spends her last year at Redmond

· Golden Jubilee of Queen Victoria

· Sir Arthur Conan Doyle publishes the first Sherlock Holmes story

——————————— 1888 ———————————

Anne is twenty-two years old; she graduates from Redmond; she refuses Roy Gardner; Gilbert proposes again and Anne accepts; Gilbert begins medical school; Anne accepts the principalship of Summerside High School

· Kodak introduces the box camera

· Irving Berlin, American composer of "White Christmas," is born

· Katherine Mansfield, author of *The Garden Party*, is born in Wellington, New Zealand

Queen Victoria

1889

Anne is twenty-three years old; she spends her second year at Summerside and Windy Poplars

- Alfred Tennyson's "Crossing the Bar," one of Captain Jim's favourite poems, is published
- The Eiffel Tower is erected in Paris
- Charlie Chaplin, famous comedian, is born

1890

Anne is twenty-four years old; she spends her third year at Summerside and Windy Poplars

- Peanut butter is invented by a St. Louis doctor
- The first electric range is introduced
- L.M. Montgomery goes to Prince Albert, Saskatchewan, to live with her father for a year

---

1891

Anne is twenty-five years old; Anne and Gilbert are married and move to their House of Dreams in Four Winds Harbour

- Telephone service begins in "Avonlea" (Cavendish, P.E.I.)
- John Naismith introduces basketball

1892

Anne is twenty-six years old; her first child, Joyce, is born and dies the same day.

- Sir James Dewar invents the vacuum Thermos bottle
- The first electric room heater is invented in England by R.E. Crompton and J.H. Dowsing

---

1893

Anne is twenty-seven years old; Anne's second child, Jem, is born; Captain Jim dies; Anne and Gilbert move to Ingleside

- Cole Porter, American composer, is born
- The Ferris wheel and Cracker Jacks are introduced at the Chicago World's Fair
- The "Happy Birthday" tune is composed
- *Vogue* magazine is launched

Charlie Chaplin

John Naismith

Norman Rockwell

Babe Ruth

Amelia Earhart

—————— 1894 ——————

Anne is twenty-eight years old; Walter is born

• Rudyard Kipling's *Jungle Book* is published

• Norman Rockwell, American artist, is born.

—————— 1895 ——————

Anne is twenty-nine years old

• Babe Ruth, American baseball player, is born

• "Waltzing Matilda," the popular Australian ballad, is composed by A.B. "Banjo" Paterson

—————— 1896 ——————

Anne is thirty years old; the twins, Nan and Di, are born

• Gold is discovered in the Klondike in the Canadian Yukon

• Fannie Farmer publishes the first cookbook using standard measurements

• The first motion picture is shown publicly in New York City

• The first Olympic Games since the fourth century are held in Athens, Greece

• The first Nobel prizes are awarded

• The tea-bag is patented by A.V. Smith in England

—————— 1897 ——————

Anne is thirty-one years old

• The Diamond Jubilee of Queen Victoria

• Amelia Earhart, the first woman to fly solo across the Atlantic, is born

• The first comic strip ("The Katzenjammer Kids") appears in the New York *Journal*

• "Yes, Virginia, There Is a Santa Claus" editorial is published in the New York *Sun*

• Bram Stoker's *Dracula* is published

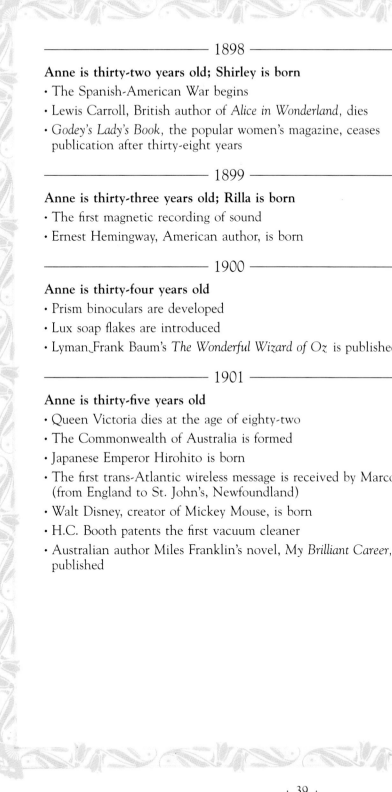

——————————— 1898 ———————————

Anne is thirty-two years old; Shirley is born
· The Spanish-American War begins
· Lewis Carroll, British author of *Alice in Wonderland*, dies
· *Godey's Lady's Book*, the popular women's magazine, ceases publication after thirty-eight years

——————————— 1899 ———————————

Anne is thirty-three years old; Rilla is born
· The first magnetic recording of sound
· Ernest Hemingway, American author, is born

——————————— 1900 ———————————

Anne is thirty-four years old
· Prism binoculars are developed
· Lux soap flakes are introduced
· Lyman Frank Baum's *The Wonderful Wizard of Oz* is published

——————————— 1901 ———————————

Anne is thirty-five years old
· Queen Victoria dies at the age of eighty-two
· The Commonwealth of Australia is formed
· Japanese Emperor Hirohito is born
· The first trans-Atlantic wireless message is received by Marconi (from England to St. John's, Newfoundland)
· Walt Disney, creator of Mickey Mouse, is born
· H.C. Booth patents the first vacuum cleaner
· Australian author Miles Franklin's novel, *My Brilliant Career*, is published

Walt Disney

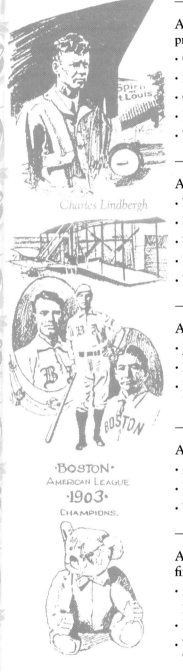

Charles Lindbergh

·BOSTON·
AMERICAN LEAGUE
·1903·
CHAMPIONS.

───────── 1902 ─────────

Anne is thirty-six years old; she becomes seriously ill with pneumonia
· Coronation of King Edward VII
· Edward Elgar composes "Pomp and Circumstance"
· Charles Lindbergh, American aviator, is born
· Beatrix Potter's *Peter Rabbit* is published
· The National Biscuit Company introduces animal crackers

───────── 1903 ─────────

Anne is thirty-seven years old
· The Wright Brothers fly at Kitty Hawk, North Carolina
· Kate Douglas Wiggin's *Rebecca of Sunnybrook Farm* is published
· The first World Series baseball game is played
· Binney and Smith begin manufacturing Crayola crayons
· The teddy bear is introduced

───────── 1904 ─────────

Anne is thirty-eight years old
· James Barrie's *Peter Pan* is published
· Laura Lee Hope's first Bobbsey Twins book is published
· Ice-cream cones and iced tea are introduced at the St. Louis World's Fair

───────── 1905 ─────────

Anne is thirty-nine years old
· Albert Einstein formulates the Theory of Relativity
· Rayon yarn is produced commercially
· The first neon sign appears

───────── 1906 ─────────

Anne is forty years old; Anne and Gilbert celebrate their fifteenth wedding anniversary
· An earthquake in San Francisco, California, kills seven hundred people
· Earl Richardson manufactures the first electric irons
· The term "hot dog" is put into use by newspaper cartoonist Thomas Aloysius Dorgan ("TAD")

—————————————— 1907 ——————————————

Anne is forty-one years old; Anne and Gilbert tour Europe; the Blythe children meet the Meredith children and begin their adventures together in Rainbow Valley

- Mother's Day is established
- Kellogg's Corn Flakes are introduced
- The Ziegfeld Follies debuts in New York

—————————————— 1908 ——————————————

Anne is forty-two years old

- Kenneth Grahame's *The Wind in the Willows* is published
- Lord Baden-Powell founds the Boy Scouts and Girl Guides
- Henry Ford issues the first "Model T" automobile
- The Automobile Act forbids the use of motor vehicles on P.E.I. until the end of World War I
- Hugh Moore invents the disposable paper cup
- L. M. Montgomery's *Anne of Green Gables* is published

—————————————— 1909 ——————————————

Anne is forty-three years old

- Admiral Robert Peary becomes the first person the reach the North Pole
- The International Boundary Waters Convention between Canada and the U.S. is signed
- L.M. Montgomery's *Anne of Avonlea* is published

—————————————— 1910 ——————————————

Anne is forty-four years old

- Halley's Comet appears
- King Edward VII dies
- Florence Nightingale dies
- The first Father's Day is observed
- Westinghouse introduces the first electric toaster

Admiral Robert Peary

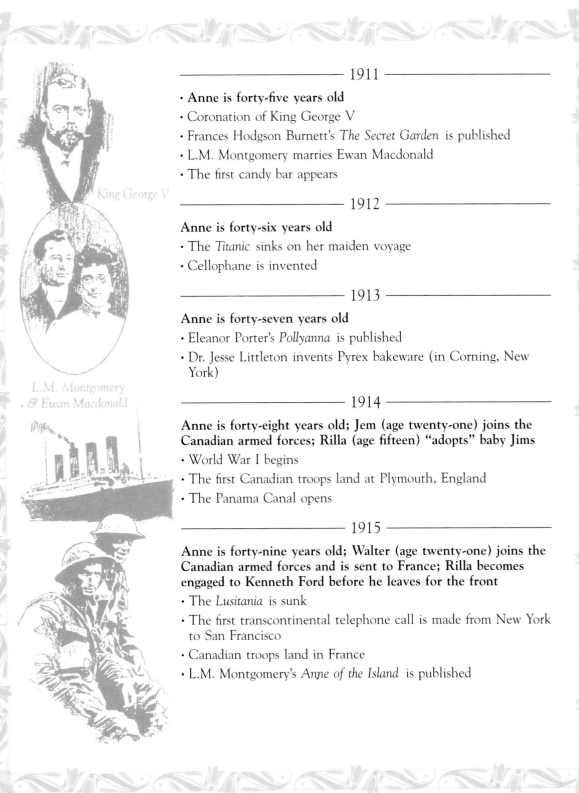

King George V

L.M. Montgomery
& Ewan Macdonald

———————— 1911 ————————

· **Anne is forty-five years old**
· Coronation of King George V
· Frances Hodgson Burnett's *The Secret Garden* is published
· L.M. Montgomery marries Ewan Macdonald
· The first candy bar appears

———————— 1912 ————————

Anne is forty-six years old
· The *Titanic* sinks on her maiden voyage
· Cellophane is invented

———————— 1913 ————————

Anne is forty-seven years old
· Eleanor Porter's *Pollyanna* is published
· Dr. Jesse Littleton invents Pyrex bakeware (in Corning, New York)

———————— 1914 ————————

Anne is forty-eight years old; Jem (age twenty-one) joins the Canadian armed forces; Rilla (age fifteen) "adopts" baby Jims
· World War I begins
· The first Canadian troops land at Plymouth, England
· The Panama Canal opens

———————— 1915 ————————

Anne is forty-nine years old; Walter (age twenty-one) joins the Canadian armed forces and is sent to France; Rilla becomes engaged to Kenneth Ford before he leaves for the front
· The *Lusitania* is sunk
· The first transcontinental telephone call is made from New York to San Francisco
· Canadian troops land in France
· L.M. Montgomery's *Anne of the Island* is published

1916

Anne is fifty years old; Walter is killed at Courcelette
- The Houses of Parliament at Ottawa are destroyed by fire
- Full rail-ferry service from P.E.I. to the Canadian mainland begins
- Nail polish is introduced

1917

Anne is fifty-one years old; Shirley (age nineteen) joins the Canadian armed forces; Gilbert buys the Blythes' first automobile
- The United States enters World War I
- Johnny Gruell's first Raggedy Ann stories are published
- E.W. Cox invents S.O.S. soap pads
- L.M. Montgomery's *Anne's House of Dreams* is published

1918

- **Anne is fifty-two years old; Jem is "wounded and missing"**
- World War I ends
- Daylight Savings Time is introduced in Canada
- Leonard Bernstein, American composer and conductor, is born

1919

Anne is fifty-three years old; Jem returns from Europe
- Sir Edmund Hillary, first to reach the summit of Mt. Everest, is born
- Lady Astor is the first woman elected to the British Parliament
- L.M. Montgomery's *Rainbow Valley* is published

Sir Edmund Hillary

CHAPTER 4

School Days, Special Days

"New worlds of thought, feeling, and ambition, fresh, fascinating fields of unexplored knowledge seemed to be opening out before Anne's eager eyes."
(ANNE OF GREEN GABLES, XXXI)

Anne did not attend school regularly until she came to Green Gables, though she had read everything she could find and learned poetry "off by heart," even as a young child. But she was naturally curious ("how are you going to find out about things if you don't ask questions?") and smart, so once she began going to the Avonlea school, she did very well at her studies.

Anne stayed at the head of her class for several reasons. She had her own strong need to excel, and she wanted Marilla, and especially Matthew, to be proud of her (she loved "to see Matthew's kindly brown eyes gleam with pride in her achievement"). And, of course, her rivalry with Gilbert Blythe gave her the extra push she sometimes needed to stay at the top.

Like most children who lived in rural communities in Canada and the United States during the late 1800s, Anne attended a one-room schoolhouse where children from the surrounding area were taught by one teacher. There were eight grades, and children went to school from age seven to age fifteen or sixteen.

The Avonlea school was "a whitewashed building…furnished inside with comfortable substantial old-fashioned desks that opened and shut, and were carved all over their lids with the initials and hieroglyphics of three generations of schoolchildren." Long rows of wooden desks, graduated in size, were bolted to the floor; two students sat at each desk. A blackboard stretched across the front wall of the room, with the teacher's desk and chair on a platform in front of it. A portrait of Queen Victoria, the ruling monarch at that time, was displayed over the blackboard, and the British flag stood in one corner (the Canadian maple leaf flag was not adopted until 1965). A large black heating stove was located at the back of the room – one of the teacher's duties was to get a fire started in it on cold mornings.

While paper or notebooks and pencil or pen and ink were used for work that had to be turned in to the teacher, students used slates and chalk for practising their handwriting, spelling, arithmetic exercises and drawing. Anne used her slate for another purpose when Gilbert Blythe teased her about her hair:

Thwack! Anne had brought her slate down on Gilbert's head and cracked it – the slate, not head – clear across. (ANNE OF GREEN GABLES, XV)

Of course, this was too much for the teacher, Mr. Phillips, who believed that order in the classroom was all-important. He commanded Anne "to stand on the platform in front of the blackboard for the rest of the afternoon," and he inscribed on the blackboard, "Ann Shirley has a very bad temper. Ann Shirley must learn to control her temper." Humiliation was one of the most frequent punishments that teachers like Mr. Phillips used for students who misbehaved. Standing in front of the class, being kept in at recess, copying and recopying phrases were usually enough to convince most students to behave acceptably, but physical punishment was sometimes used. Even Anne, who had said she would never whip a student when she became a teacher, finally resorted to the use of a heavy wooden pointer when she lost her temper with her most difficult student on a particularly bad school day. However, her conscience tortured her afterwards, for she felt she had failed to "govern by affection."

Even though the setting was a humble one, the curriculum in the one-room school was rigorous. At age eleven Anne was studying reading, geography, history, spelling and grammar, arithmetic, penmanship, some science and drawing. By the end of her first term she was allowed to begin studying Latin, geometry, French and algebra as well. The only subject she seemed to have real trouble with was geometry. "It is casting a cloud over my whole life," she said once. "I'm such a dunce at it."

In Canada, the basic textbooks in those years were the Royal Readers, which were similar to the McGuffey Eclectic Readers used by most children in the United States. The readers contained stories and poems on a variety of subjects, so that while the students were learning to read, write and spell, they were also learning about literature, history, science and the lives of famous people. The readers taught moral values as well – many of the passages stressed courage, generosity, humility, honesty, loyalty, performance of duty and resisting temptation.

In addition to the Royal Readers, there were textbooks for composition, arithmetic, history, grammar, geography, bookkeeping, music, drawing, English literature, natural philosophy, physiology, botany, chemistry, physics, astronomy, geology, algebra, geometry, trigonometry, French, Latin and Greek. Just imagine being a teacher and having to teach all of these subjects to a roomful of students of assorted ages and grade levels!

Anne began to study for the entrance examinations to Teachers' College when she was thirteen years old and in grade seven. At the end of grade eight, she and the other applicants wrote six examinations over three days. Because of the extra studying with

Miss Stacy and her own determination to do well, Anne finished first out of two hundred, and that fall she enrolled at Queen's Academy in Charlottetown to begin her studies to become a teacher. Her tuition would have been seven dollars for the year. (L.M. Montgomery used her alma mater, Prince of Wales College, as the model for "Queen's" in the Anne books.)

Most students studied the first year for a second-class teaching licence, then studied a second year for a first-class licence. Anne, however, decided to aim for a first-class licence in her first year, although this meant she had twice the academic load. A first-class teaching licence was not only more prestigious; it meant a higher salary as well. At that time, the average annual salary for female teachers of the first class was $360 (male teachers received about $100 more).

At the end of the school year, Anne took the examinations for her first-class licence. There were forty hours of exams covering sixteen subjects, including Latin, Greek, algebra, geometry, French, English, chemistry and music. Anne not only passed, but was at the top of her class and was awarded the Avery Scholarship, which would later pay her college tuition.

Although Anne had planned to attend Redmond College after completing her teaching course at Queen's, she changed her plans when Matthew died suddenly. She decided to stay with Marilla in Avonlea and teach in the same one-room school where she had been a student. She was only sixteen when she began teaching – not much older than her pupils! When Mrs. Lynde came to live with Marilla two years later, Anne was able to go to Redmond College for four years. She was then offered the post of principal of Summerside High School, and she taught there while Gilbert studied for his medical degree. Her teaching career ended when they were married, for it was the custom then for married women to devote their time to the many duties at home.

Anne's schooling and teaching careers bore many similarities to L.M. Montgomery's. Both attended one-room schools and were very

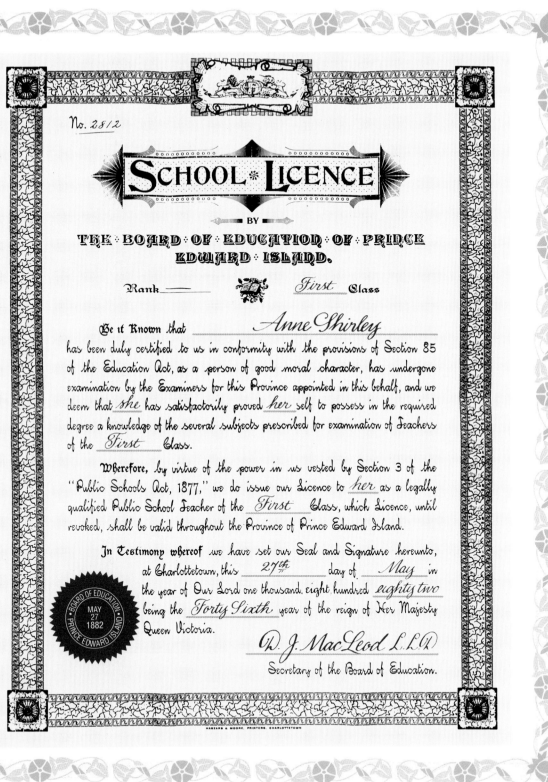

No. 2812

SCHOOL · LICENCE

BY

THE · BOARD · OF · EDUCATION · OF · PRINCE · EDWARD · ISLAND.

Rank ——— *First* Class

Be it Known that *Anne Shirley*

has been duly certified to us in conformity with the provisions of Section 85 of the Education Act, as a person of good moral character, has undergone examination by the Examiners for this Province appointed in this behalf, and we deem that *she* has satisfactorily proved *her* self to possess in the required degree a knowledge of the several subjects prescribed for examination of Teachers of the *First* Class.

Wherefore, by virtue of the power in us vested by Section 3 of the "Public Schools Act, 1877," we do issue our Licence to *her* as a legally qualified Public School Teacher of the *First* Class, which Licence, until revoked, shall be valid throughout the Province of Prince Edward Island.

In Testimony whereof we have set our Seal and Signature hereunto, at Charlottetown, this *27th* day of *May* in the year of Our Lord one thousand, eight hundred *eighty two* being the *Forty Sixth* year of the reign of Her Majesty Queen Victoria.

D. J. MacLeod L.L.D
Secretary of the Board of Education.

BOARD OF EDUCATION
MAY 27 1882
PRINCE EDWARD ISLAND

HASZARD & MOORE, PRINTERS, CHARLOTTETOWN.

good students who loved poetry passionately. Both became teachers, and both felt duty-bound to interrupt their studies in order to stay at home with elderly relatives – Anne with Marilla and Maud with her grandmother.

The one-room school with one teacher for all grades continued to be the way children in rural areas were educated until the 1920s, when better roads and motor vehicles began to make it possible for school districts to bring students from outlying areas to larger and more modern schools. But *Anne of Green Gables* would have been a very different story if Anne had gone to a modern school – she wouldn't have had a slate to crack over Gilbert's head, or the daily walks to and from school through Violet Vale and Lover's Lane. And the milk for lunches would have been kept cool in a refrigerator instead of the brook behind the schoolyard!

* * *

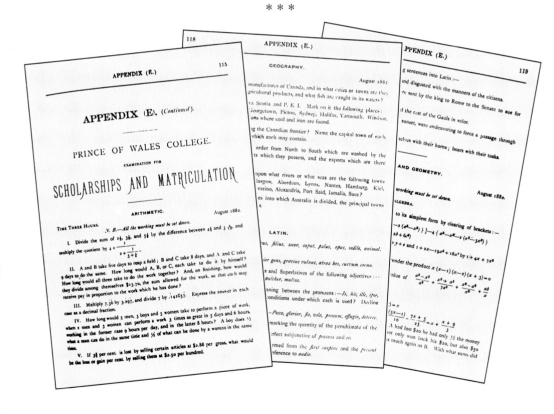

While studying took up much of Anne's time, and there were always chores to be done at Green Gables, there was still a surprising amount of free time as well. Of course, there were no radios, televisions or movies in those days, and there were not very many toys for children to play with, either. So Anne and her friends had to create their own entertainment.

In the summer months, Anne and Diana spent many wonderful hours outdoors, roaming the woods and fields around Avonlea and making friends with every tree, shrub, path and brook around Green Gables and Orchard Slope. They would visit their favourite places often and would make up stories about fairies and enchanted princesses.

Another of Anne's summertime entertainments was to get together with girlfriends to act out some of their favourite poems and stories that they had learned at school. On one unforgettable summer afternoon, they dramatized a scene from Tennyson's *Idylls of the King*, in which Elaine, the lily maid, floats down the river to Camelot. As Elaine, Anne arranged herself in Mr. Barry's old dory, but as she began the trip downstream, she found herself sinking into the deep water and nearly drowning – quite a different ending from the romantic scene she had imagined!

In addition to these everyday pleasures, summer also brought a number of special occasions, from tea parties and Sunday School picnics to the highlight – the Charlottetown Exhibition. The Exhibition was similar to the county and state fairs we have today, with horse races, fortune-telling and displays of handiwork, fruits and vegetables, flowers and animals. Prizes were given for the most outstanding items in each class – Miss Cornelia Bryant won first prize at the 1881 Exhibition for her lemon pie (she never made any more, however, "for fear of losing her reputation for them"), and Susan Baker captured first prize for her crocheted lace in 1905.

Despite the cold and periodic snowstorms, winters at Green Gables also included more than school and chores. In fact, it was actually easier to visit with neighbours during the winter months, because there was more free time (planting, harvesting and preparing food for storage took up most of the time in the warmer months), and travel was easier. In winter, the muddy, rutted roads that were so difficult for buggies and wagons to travel were frozen and covered with a packed layer of snow, which sleighs could glide over much more easily.

One favourite community activity, especially during the winter, was the "concert," which included music, but also featured members of the community in recitations of dramatic poems and dialogues. Anne went to her first concert when she was eleven, after she managed to convince Marilla that the evening would be worthwhile. (There would be "four lovely pathetic songs that are pretty near as good as hymns…" she told Marilla, and the minister would "give an address. That will be just about the same thing as a sermon.") Anne particularly thrilled to the recitations of poems that told of heroism and tragic death (preferably of a broken heart!).

Most of the social occasions in Anne's day were combined with productive activities. Concerts entertained as well as trained participants in memorization techniques and public speaking. They also featured selections that were considered desirable for their high moral content, reinforcing lessons learned at school and church. Quilting parties gave the women of the community several hours to talk together while finishing two or three quilts, perhaps for giving to a bride for her new home, or to charity. And in a settlement such as Avonlea, almost everyone went to church and took an active part in its many programs – morning and evening services on Sundays and various meetings during the week (L.M. Montgomery herself was organist at the Cavendish Presbyterian Church for many years).

Other celebrations centred on the principal holidays. Victoria Day was set aside to celebrate the birthday of Queen Victoria (May 24), who ruled the British Empire from 1837 to 1901. Anne and Diana honoured the occasion in 1878 by naming a new island they had found in the brook that day "Victoria Island."

Canada Day, also known as Confederation Day and Dominion Day, celebrates the "birthday" of Canada. It was proclaimed on July 1, 1867, when the provinces of Ontario, Quebec, New Brunswick and Nova Scotia joined to form the Dominion of Canada. It has always been an occasion for all-day picnics, parades, concerts and fireworks. Today it is observed on the first of July.

Thanksgiving was first declared a national holiday in Canada in 1879 (when Anne was thirteen years old) and, until 1900, was celebrated in November, despite Anne's opinion that it would be better celebrated in the spring ("…I think it would be ever so much better than having it in November when everything is dead or asleep. Then you have to remember to be thankful; but in May one simply can't help being thankful… that they are alive, if for nothing else.") Today the official Canadian Thanksgiving Day is the second Monday in October.

And of course Anne spent many memorable Christmases at Green Gables. Her second Christmas there was a particularly special one, marked by a treasured present from Matthew – the long-hoped-for dress with puffed sleeves – and her first appearance in a concert. Later Christmases featured long walks and talks with Diana and Gilbert and other Avonlea friends, moonlit "snowshoe tramps" through the woods and fields, ice-skating on the frozen streams and ponds, sleigh rides, bonfires, parties and concerts, along with trimming the tree, exchanging gifts and sampling special holiday treats that filled the Green Gables pantry.

In between the holidays and other special-occasion days of the year were those days Anne came to like best – days when nothing "very splendid or wonderful or exciting" happened, but were a happy mixture of household tasks and lessons, daydreams and bits of fun.

CHAPTER 5

Tea Time

"Tea first…what do you want for tea? We'll have whatever you like. Do think of something nice and indigestible." (ANNE OF AVONLEA, XXIII)

The custom of serving tea was brought to Canada by the many immigrants from Great Britain, where the tea-time ritual began and was refined and, thankfully, continues to this day. In the Anne books, tea was any meal eaten after mid-afternoon, whether it was a snack, light supper or substantial dinner. When it was a formal occasion, Anne and her friends treated tea with great seriousness.

…Diana came over, dressed in her second best dress and looking exactly as it is proper to look when asked out to tea. At other times she was wont to run into the kitchen without knocking; but now she knocked primly at the front door. And when Anne, dressed in her second best, as primly opened it, both little girls shook hands as gravely as if they had never met before. This unnatural solemnity lasted until after Diana had been taken to the east gable to lay off her hat and then had sat for ten minutes in the sitting room, toes in position. (ANNE OF GREEN GABLES, XVI)

The teas that are described most fully in the Anne books are of the special-occasion variety that consisted of treats such as sandwiches, fresh or preserved fruits, cheese, breads, cookies, cakes, pies, tarts and other desserts. A "splendid tea," as Anne described one of her Sunday School picnics, would have included those kinds of dishes as well as more substantial fare—meats, salads and vegetables. Extra-special treats such as ice cream assured the success of such occasions.

The scene of many happy tea times for Anne and Diana was Echo Lodge—Miss Lavendar Lewis's cottage hidden deep in the forest. On their very first chance visit to the remote cottage, the young ladies were fascinated to discover that Miss Lavendar had prepared an elaborate tea, with the table "…set out with pale blue china and laden with delicacies, while little golden-hued ferns scattered over the cloth gave it what Anne would have termed 'a festal air.'"

It turned out that Miss Lavendar and her hired girl, Charlotta the Fourth, were pretending to have guests to help themselves over their feelings of loneliness. How happy they were when Anne and Diana appeared at the door! Miss Lavendar persuaded the girls to stay for tea, and it was the first of many afternoons they spent together at the little stone house, "cooking and feasting and making candy and laughing and 'pretending'" and enjoying each other's company.

Planning an Anne Tea Party

Tea always tastes best when it is shared. Why not invite a few of your friends over for a tea party, serving some of the treats from the Anne books? Getting ready for the party is almost as much fun as the party itself, for you'll have a wonderful excuse to prepare a beautiful table setting, serve an array of delicious tidbits, perhaps dress up a little, and have a "perfectly scrumptious time," as Anne might say.

Anne first entertained for tea in her first year at Green Gables. Marilla was to be out but gave Anne permission to invite Diana over for the afternoon. Marilla didn't allow Anne to go as far as to use the rosebud spray tea set, which was reserved for the most honoured of guests, but she did offer to let Anne serve cherry preserves, fruit cake, cookies and snaps – and raspberry cordial. More important to Anne than the menu, however, was creating just the right atmosphere for such a grown-up activity as having a friend for tea.

"I can just imagine myself sitting down at the head of the table and pouring out the tea," said Anne ecstatically. "And asking Diana if she takes sugar! I know she doesn't but of course I'll ask her just as if I didn't know. And then pressing her to take another piece of fruitcake and another helping of preserves. Oh, Marilla, it's a wonderful sensation just to think of it." (ANNE OF GREEN GABLES, XVI)

Though the afternoon ended in an unorthodox way, Anne and Diana observed the most important elements of proper tea-time behaviour – special attention to one's grooming and clothes, polite but sincere conversation, exquisite manners, an attractive table setting, and an appealing variety of foods offered with the tea itself.

You may decide only to serve a plate of sandwiches or cookies at tea, but if you want to prepare an extra-special occasion, you can serve one or more "courses." The following tea-time treats are mentioned in the Anne books, and you might want to try some of them for your own tea party.

Brewing the Perfect Pot of Tea

Learning to prepare tea properly is one of the first steps in bringing Anne's world into your own.

First, there are three main types of tea – black, oolong (semi-black) and green. Black tea is fermented before it is dried; green tea is steamed but not fermented before it is dried; and oolong is fermented only briefly before it is dried. Anne and her friends drank black tea (such as to-day's English Breakfast or Irish Breakfast), which was the most common tea in the Canadian Maritimes. It is served at any time of day, while the more exotic oolong and green teas are reserved for the after-noon or evening.

Tea is a delicate beverage, and to coax the subtleties of taste and aroma from the leaves, you must observe a few simple but basic rules.

1 Run enough fresh, cold water into a tea kettle to fill the tea pot, plus an extra cup or two. Bring it just to a rolling boil.

2 While the water is heating, fill the tea pot with hot water; this will enable the pot to keep the tea hot much longer. Just before the boiling water is ready, pour the hot water out of the tea pot.

3 To the pot, add 1 tsp (5 mL) tea leaves for each tea cup – ¾ cup (175 mL) – of water. The average tea pot will hold four to six tea cupfuls, so you will need 4 to 6 tsp (20 to 30 mL) tea.

4 Pour boiling water over the tea leaves in the pot, stir gently and place the lid on the pot. Allow the tea to "steep" or stand for 3 to 5 minutes, stir again and serve immediately, pouring the tea through a strainer into the tea cups. The strainer will keep the loose tea leaves out of the tea cups. (Some people like to strain the brewed tea into *another* heated tea pot before serving, so there will be no loose tea leaves to deal with and the tea will not get any stronger. But you can simply have more hot water on hand; if you want to heat up or dilute the tea a bit, add a little hot water to the tea in the cup.)

5 Serve the tea with sugar and thinly sliced lemon or milk.

Since the tea bag was not invented until 1896, it is highly unlikely that Anne used it. While the tea bag is a convenient method of brewing tea, the tea leaves do not open enough to brew properly when they are confined to such cramped quarters, and the material of the tea bag itself can impart its own flavour to the tea.

There are other beverages mentioned in the Anne books – Marilla's raspberry cordial (made from fresh raspberries, sugar, vinegar and water), homemade currant wine, ginger tea, Anne's Golden Picnic lemonade, Miss Minerva Tomgallon's cocoa, and even coffee, which was considered exotic enough then to be included in the luncheon menu for Mrs. Charlotte Morgan – but the beverage most often served was tea.

First Course: Sandwiches

"We must have sandwiches too, though they're not very poetical." (ANNE OF AVONLEA, XIII)

A variety of tiny sandwiches served with the first cup of tea is a fitting beginning for any tea party. Finely textured white bread is most often used for tea sandwiches, but you can also choose whole wheat or light rye or a combination of breads. Slice the bread as thinly as you can – about ¼-inch (5-mm) slices are ideal.

Butter the slices on one side and spread your choice of fillings on one of the slices (the filling can be about as thick as the bread slice or a little less) and top with a second slice of bread. Now carefully trim the crusts from the bread and cut the sandwich into three rectangles or four triangles. You can even use scalloped or heart-shaped cookie cutters to add a more "poetical" touch if you like. Make enough little sandwiches so that each person can have three or four. Arrange them on an attractive plate or platter, and garnish with parsley sprigs if you have them.

Chicken salad, thinly sliced cucumbers, watercress, herbed cream cheese, egg salad, thinly sliced meats and cheese all make wonderful sandwiches for tea. Even simple bread and butter, butter and jam or peanut butter and jelly sandwiches are fine.

Make your sandwiches as close to tea time as possible, but if you need to make them a few hours ahead of time, cover them with a slightly damp tea towel (as Anne would have done) or plastic wrap and keep them in the refrigerator until you are ready to serve.

CHICKEN SALAD SANDWICHES

Chicken salad was considered especially elegant in Anne's day – it was served at nearly every wedding reception, including Anne's, though then it would have been mounded on lettuce leaves and eaten with a fork.

Make sure all the filling ingredients are chopped into very small pieces; otherwise your sandwiches will be too thick and will fall apart when you try to cut them into shapes.

Remember, if you are not going to serve the sandwiches right away, keep them in the refrigerator, covered with a dampened tea towel or plastic wrap.

1 cup	finely chopped cooked chicken	250 mL
¼ cup	finely chopped celery	50 mL
1	hard-boiled egg, peeled and finely chopped	1
1 tbsp	finely chopped sweet pickle or sweet pickle relish	15 mL
1 tsp	finely chopped green onion	5 mL
2 to 3 tbsp	mayonnaise	25 to 45 mL
	Salt and pepper to taste	
6	thin slices bread	6
	Butter, at room temperature	

1 In a bowl, mix together the chicken, celery, egg, pickle and green onion. Stir in the mayonnaise until you have a nice moist mixture. Add salt and pepper to taste. Keep the mixture in the refrigerator, covered, until you are ready to make the sandwiches.

2 Butter each slice of bread on one side. Spread the filling on three of the buttered slices and top with the remaining slices of bread. Trim the crusts off the sandwiches and cut each sandwich into shapes.

Makes 3 whole sandwiches

CREAM CHEESE SANDWICHES

Anne undoubtedly helped Marilla make cream cheese from some of the milk from the Green Gables cows. They would have used the cream cheese for all sorts of wonderful treats, including sandwiches.

If you are using the modern whipped cream cheese, you may not need to add the milk.

4 oz	softened cream cheese	125 g
2 tsp	milk	10 mL
2 tbsp	finely chopped dates, raisins, dried apricots, or green olives, *or*	25 mL
2 tsp	finely chopped green onions	10 mL
6	thin slices bread	6

1 In a bowl, mix together the softened cream cheese and milk until the mixture is smooth. Add your choice of dried fruit, olives or onions and stir them in.

2 Spread the filling on three slices of bread and top with the remaining slices. Trim off the crusts and cut the sandwiches into shapes.

Makes 3 whole sandwiches

CUCUMBER OR WATERCRESS SANDWICHES

Cucumbers (or "cowcumbers," as Miss Sarah Copp of Spencervale called them) were grown in most kitchen gardens in Anne's day. They can be sliced and eaten fresh in salads and sandwiches, or they can be pickled.

Watercress grows beside rivers, streams or brooks, in cool places. It is easy to imagine Anne running down to the stream between Green Gables and Orchard Slope to gather a bunch of watercress for a salad, soup, or to make elegant sandwiches for tea!

1 Spread a thin layer of softened cream cheese or butter on a piece of thinly sliced bread and top with paper-thin slices of cucumber or sprigs of watercress. Top with another piece of bread, trim off the crusts and cut into desired shapes. Decorate each tiny sandwich with a bit of parsley or a watercress leaf.

PEANUT BUTTER AND JELLY SANDWICHES

Even though Anne did not grow up with peanut butter and jelly sandwiches (peanut butter wasn't even invented until she was twenty-four), it is perfectly possible that her six children persuaded her to include this now classic sandwich on the tea-time trays of Ingleside!

1 Spread a thin layer of creamy-style peanut butter on one side of a piece of thinly sliced bread. On a second slice of bread, spread your favourite jelly, jam or honey. Put the two slices together (with their fillings on the inside!), trim off the crusts and cut into desired shapes.

Second Course: Biscuits, Butter and Jam

When they went down Miss Lavendar was carrying in the tea pot, and behind her, looking vastly pleased, was Charlotta the Fourth, with a plate of hot biscuits. (ANNE OF AVONLEA, XXI)

After the sandwiches, offer your guests more tea and some hot biscuits with butter and jam. If the tea is disappearing or cooling down too much, perhaps you should start another kettle of water boiling for a second pot. No tea party hostess should run out of tea!

TEA BISCUITS

Mrs. Rachel and Marilla sat comfortably in the parlour while Anne got the tea and made hot biscuits that were light and white enough to defy even Mrs. Rachel's criticism. (ANNE OF GREEN GABLES, XXX)

To make sure your biscuits are as light as Anne's, mix in the milk with quick light strokes and treat the dough gently when you are patting it out.

For fun, you might try cutting out tiny biscuits with a thimble, as little Elizabeth Grayson did when she visited Green Gables with Anne one summer. After cutting out your regular-sized biscuits, pat the remaining dough down until it is about ¼ inch (5 mm) thick and cut tiny biscuits. A doughnut-hole cutter could be substituted for the thimble.

1 ¼ cups	all-purpose flour	300 mL
1 ¼ tsp	baking powder	6 mL
¼ tsp	baking soda	1 mL
pinch	salt	pinch
6 tbsp	cold butter, cut in small pieces	90 mL
6 tbsp	milk or buttermilk	90 mL

1 Preheat your oven to 400 F (200 C).

2 In a large bowl, combine the flour, baking powder, baking soda and salt.

3 Add the butter to the dry ingredients and, using a pastry blender, your fingers or a fork, blend it in thoroughly until the mixture has the look of coarse crumbs.

4 Add the milk and mix it in just until blended.

5 Turn the dough out onto a lightly floured board. Flour your hands and pat out the dough until it is about ½ inch (1.25 cm) thick.

6 Cut out biscuits with a 1½-inch (3.75-cm) floured cutter. (Do not twist the cutter.) Place the biscuits about ½ inch (1.25 cm) apart on an ungreased baking sheet.

7 Bake the biscuits for 10 to 12 minutes, or until they are just golden-brown. Butter the tops of the biscuits lightly as soon as they come out of the oven. Serve them hot, if possible, with butter and jam.

Makes about 16 biscuits

WILLOW-WARE PLATTER STRAWBERRY JAM

Much to her delight, she saw, as she peered through the pane, a willow-ware platter, exactly such as she was in quest of, on the shelf in front of the window. (ANNE OF AVONLEA, XVIII)

"Willow-ware" was first produced in 1780 in England, as a result of an infatuation at that time with anything Chinese. The popular pattern, which is still being produced today, illustrates a romantic Chinese fable. In a garden featuring a large willow tree, a pagoda and a stream, two young lovers are being pursued by the girl's father, who is trying to stop them from eloping. Suddenly, the couple change into bluebirds and fly away together.

An old-fashioned method for making jam (and one Anne and Marilla very likely used from time to time) is to let the cooked jam cool and thicken on a large platter before spooning it into a jam pot. Use the jam with tea biscuits as well as in peanut butter and jelly sandwiches (page 63) or jelly-tart cookies (page 71). The recipe can easily be doubled to yield about 4 cups (1 L) jam.

2 cups	strawberries (1 pint)	500 mL
1 ¾ cups	granulated sugar	425 mL

1 Wash the strawberries, hull them, and cut away any bruised spots.

2 In a large, heavy-bottomed saucepan or Dutch oven, combine the strawberries and sugar. Crush the berries slightly with a fork or potato masher. Cook and stir, over gentle heat, until the sugar melts.

3 Raise the heat and boil the mixture for 15 to 20 minutes, until the jam changes from bright red to a darker red and thickens. Stir the jam frequently to prevent sticking or scorching. Skim off any pink foam and discard it.

4 Spoon the jam onto a large platter and let cool. Cover the jam with waxed paper or cheesecloth and let it stand for 24 hours.

5 Pour the jam into a sterilized jar. Store in the refrigerator.

Makes about 2 cups (500 mL)

Third Course: Cookies and Fruitcake

Don't forget to keep an eye on the tea; you might need to start *another* pot!

The cookies and fruitcake course is perhaps the most delightful of the four courses you are serving, because you can make all sorts of fanciful and delectable cookies. You can cut them into heart shapes or animal shapes, frost them with coloured icings, or add a bit of decoration such as coloured sugar sprinkles or nuts.

There are quite a few cookies mentioned in the Anne books – gingersnaps, lady fingers and "drop cookies frosted with pink and yellow icing," macaroons, butterscotch cookies and spice cookies. Any of these, as well as the cookies given on the following pages, would be ideal for your tea party.

SHORTBREAD

"Of course I'll stay to tea," said Anne gaily. "I was dying to be asked. My mouth has been watering for some more of your grandma's delicious shortbread ever since I had tea here before." (ANNE OF AVONLEA, XIX)

Rich, crumbly shortbread, elegant in its simplicity, is sublime with a cup of tea.

½ cup	butter, at room temperature	125 mL
2 tbsp	granulated sugar	25 mL
¼ tsp	vanilla	1 mL
1 ¼ cups	all-purpose flour	300 mL
pinch	salt	pinch
1 tsp	granulated sugar	5 mL

1. Preheat your oven to 325 F (160 C).

2. In a large bowl, with a wooden spoon, blend together the butter, 2 tbsp (25 mL) sugar and the vanilla until the mixture is light and fluffy.

3. With a pastry cutter, wooden spoon or your fingers, mix in the flour and salt until the mixture is nice and crumbly. Squeeze the dough into a ball with your hands and put it in the middle of an ungreased baking sheet.

4. With your hands, firmly pat the dough into a 7-inch (18-cm) circle – the circle of dough should be about ½ inch (1.25 cm) thick. Prick the dough deeply with the tines of a fork so that twelve pie-shaped wedges are outlined. Sprinkle the circle of dough with 1 tsp (5 mL) sugar (coloured sugar is nice, especially at holiday time).

5. Bake the shortbread for 20 to 25 minutes, or until it is ever so slightly browned. Let the shortbread cool for 1 minute on the baking sheet, then carefully cut it into twelve wedges. Remove the wedges to a wire rack to finish cooling.

Makes 12 wedges of shortbread

LEMON BISCUITS

"There's a hot chicken pie for supper and I made some of my lemon biscuits for you."
(ANNE OF INGLESIDE, 1)

Here we believe Mrs. Rachel Lynde used the term "biscuit" to mean "cookie" rather than a scone-type biscuit.

¼ cup	butter, at room temperature	50 mL
½ cup	granulated sugar	125 mL
1	egg	1
½ tsp	grated lemon rind or lemon extract	2mL
1 cup	all-purpose flour	250 mL
¼ tsp	baking soda	1 mL
¼ tsp	cream of tartar	1 mL
pinch	salt	pinch

1 Preheat your oven to 325 F (160 C).

2 In a medium bowl, with a wooden spoon, blend the butter and sugar together until smooth and fluffy. Mix in the egg and grated lemon rind or extract.

3 In a separate bowl, combine the flour, baking soda, cream of tartar and salt. Stir the dry ingredients into the butter mixture until you have a smooth, soft dough.

4 Flour your hands and pinch off bits of dough about ½ tsp (2 mL) at a time. Roll each bit into a ball or simply drop onto an ungreased baking sheet, about 2 inches (5 cm) apart.

5 Using the bottom of a glass tumbler that has been greased and dipped in sugar, press each cookie until it is about ¼ inch (5 mm) thick.

6 Bake for about 8 minutes, or until the cookies are barely golden underneath. (These cookies are very tender. After the first 5 minutes or so, check them every minute to see that they are not overbrown.) Let the cookies cool on a wire rack.

Makes about 3 dozen cookies

MONKEY FACE COOKIES

Walter was in bed, warm, fed, comforted. Susan had whisked on a fire, got him a hot cup of milk, a slice of golden-brown toast and a big plateful of his favourite "monkey face" cookies, and then tucked him away with a hot-water bottle at his feet. (ANNE OF INGLESIDE, X)

The raisin "faces" provide a touch of whimsy to these deliciously spicy molasses cookies. Today we have the luxury of seedless raisins, but before Anne could have used raisins in a recipe, she would have had to pick out all the tiny seeds by hand!

⅓ cup	butter, at room temperature	75 mL
½ cup	granulated sugar	125 mL
1	egg	1
2 tbsp	molasses	25 mL
1 ½ cups	all-purpose flour	375 mL
1 tsp	baking soda	5 mL
pinch	salt	pinch
1 tsp	ground cinnamon	5 mL
1 tsp	ground ginger	5 mL
¼ cup	raisins or currants	50 mL

1 Preheat your oven to 350 F (180 C). Lightly grease a baking sheet.

2 In a large bowl, using a wooden spoon, blend together the butter and sugar until the mixture is light and fluffy. Stir in the egg and molasses.

3 In a separate bowl, combine the flour, baking soda, salt, cinnamon and ginger. Stir the dry ingredients into the butter/egg mixture.

4 Flour your hands and pinch off bits of dough about ½ tsp (2 mL) at a time. Roll each bit into a ball or simply drop onto the baking sheet, about 2 inches (5 cm) apart.

5 Using the bottom of a glass tumbler that has been greased and dipped in sugar, press each cookie until it is about ¼ inch (5 mm) thick. Press three raisins into each cookie to make the eyes and mouth of the "monkey face."

6 Bake the cookies for about 8 minutes, or until firm. Let the cookies cool on a wire rack.

Makes about 3 dozen cookies

JELLY-TART COOKIES

"I'm going to have the daintiest things possible...things that will match the spring, you understand...little jelly tarts and lady fingers, and drop cookies frosted with pink and yellow icing, and buttercup cake."

(ANNE OF AVONLEA, XIII)

These "little jelly tarts" are easy and fun to make and will glimmer like jewels on your tea tray. Use your favourite jam or jelly; Anne probably would have used apricot, strawberry, raspberry, or even marmalade.

¼ cup	jelly	50 mL
1 cup	butter, at room temperature	250 mL
⅓ cup	granulated sugar	75 mL
1¾ cups	all-purpose flour	425 mL
pinch	salt	pinch

1 Preheat your oven to 350 F (180 C).

2 Spoon the jelly into a small bowl and stir until it is smooth. Set aside.

3 In a large bowl, using a wooden spoon, blend together the butter and sugar until the mixture is light and fluffy.

4 In a separate bowl, mix together the flour and salt. Add the dry ingredients to the butter mixture and blend until a dough is formed.

5 Pinch off bits of dough and roll into 1-inch (2.5-cm) balls. Place the balls on a baking sheet about 1 inch (2.5 cm) apart. Press your fingertip into the centre of each cookie to make a deep little "well" (the dough may crack around the edges – you can pinch it back together if you wish). Fill each well with about ¼ tsp (1 mL) jelly.

6 Bake the cookies for about 10 minutes. Remove them to a wire rack to cool. (The jelly will be *very* hot when you take the cookies out of the oven, so handle them carefully and cool them completely before serving.)

Makes about 3 dozen cookies

FRUITCAKE

"We eat all sorts of indigestible things when-ever we happen to think of it, by day or night; and we flourish like green bay trees.... Nothing has ever killed us yet; but Char-lotta the Fourth has been known to have bad dreams after we had eaten doughnuts and mince pie and fruit cake before we went to bed." (ANNE OF AVONLEA, XXVII)

Though we are not going to include a recipe for fruitcake (would you really want to make it?!), we would like you to know a bit about it.

Homemade fruit cake was always in-cluded in the assortment of sweet treats at Miss Lavendar's tea table, as it was at most tea tables during Anne's time. The cake was usually made in the fall and stored in the pantry to be on hand for unexpected guests as well as special occasions.

In Anne's day, a rich fruitcake contain-ing candied fruits, dates, raisins, nuts and spices might be decorated in marzipan for the ultimate wedding cake. With its ex-cellent keeping qualities, the cake could be stored and brought out on succeeding anniversaries – a sentimental touch very much in keeping with that era.

There are many delicious fruitcakes available today in grocery and gourmet stores, and you can purchase one instead of going to the immense trouble and expense of making your own. Or perhaps you know someone who might have some homemade fruitcake to share with you, or even teach you how to make it!

To serve, slice the fruitcake into very thin slices, since it is extremely rich. To store the cake, wrap it well and place it in an airtight container such as a tin box. You can wrap the cake in cheesecloth that has been soaked in brandy. Pierce the cake in several places with a skewer or toothpick and, every few weeks, pour a spoonful of brandy over the cake to keep it moist and discourage mould.

Fourth Course: Desserts

You don't have to serve dessert for tea—cookies and fruitcake (or just cookies) would certainly be enough. But in the event that you would like to add one more course, here are some suggestions that should make your tea party a very memorable occasion indeed.

Pies and tarts are among the favourite dessert treats mentioned in the Anne books. Diana carried "three juicy, toothsome raspberry tarts" in her lunch basket to school one day. And of course you remember Anne's "golden circles" of lemon pies that were to be served so proudly to the famous author Mrs. Morgan, but ended up all over poor little Davy Keith when he fell into them by accident! There were also cherry pies, strawberry pies, apple pies, mince pies and cranberry pies—all made from the home-grown fruits of the kitchen gardens and orchards of Green Gables, the House of Dreams and Ingleside.

You will find recipes for these pies easily in the cookbooks on your kitchen shelf, but the caramel pie Anne had at tea with the crotchety Mrs. Douglas in Valley Road is a little more elusive.

CARAMEL PIE

"We had...a few other things, including more pie – caramel pie, I think it was. After I had eaten twice as much as was good for me, Mrs. Douglas sighed and said she feared she had nothing to tempt my appetite." (ANNE OF THE ISLAND, XXXII)

This is not a difficult recipe to make, but there should be a grown-up to supervise, at least until the water has been added to the hot browned sugar. Be sure to chill the pie completely before serving.

You can make your own pastry as Anne would have done, or buy already baked or frozen pie shells. In place of the baked pie shell you can substitute six baked tart shells. Instead of making the meringue, you can top the pie with whipped cream.

If you use an electric mixer to beat the egg whites for the meringue, it will only take a few minutes. But Anne and Marilla did not have that luxury! Hand-held egg beaters became available in the 1870s, but many cooks beat egg whites on a large platter with a fork, until they were high and stiff enough to use for meringue. This took at least twenty minutes, depending on the number of egg whites required!

3 tbsp	cornstarch	45 mL
1 ½ cups	water, divided	375 mL
2	eggs, separated	2
1 ½ cups	granulated sugar, divided	375 mL
½ cup	butter	125 mL
1 tsp	vanilla	5 mL
1	baked 8- or 9-inch (20-or 23-cm) pie shell	1
1 tbsp	granulated sugar	15 mL

1 In a bowl, dissolve the cornstarch with ¾ cup (175 mL) water. Beat the egg yolks and stir them into the cornstarch mixture. Set aside.

2 In a heavy saucepan with high sides, cook ¾ cup (175 mL) sugar over low to medium heat until it is completely melted and a golden-brown colour (increase the heat if the sugar takes a long time to melt). Add the remaining ¾ cup (175 mL) sugar, the butter, and the remaining ¾ cup (175 mL) water. (This may create a cloud of steam, so stand back while you are adding the water!).

3 Bring the mixture to a boil and stir until the butter has melted and the sugar has completely dissolved.

4 Stir the cornstarch/egg mixture into the saucepan and bring the mixture to a low boil, stirring it constantly. Continue to boil slowly until the mixture thickens, about 2 minutes.

5 Take the mixture off the heat, stir it until smooth, and let it cool. Stir in the vanilla and pour the filling into the baked pie shell.

6 To make a meringue topping for the pie, beat the egg whites until soft peaks form. Add 1 tbsp (15 mL) sugar and continue beating until stiff peaks form. Spoon the meringue on top of the pie filling, spreading it right up to the edge of the filling. Bake at 350 F (180 C) for about 15 minutes, or until the top of the meringue is delicately browned. Chill the pie before serving.

Makes one pie

CAKES

While pies were certainly a treat for Anne and her friends, cakes were even more impressive, for they were much more demanding of the cook's skill. Ingredients had to be very fresh, and measuring carefully was a bit risky, since there were no standard measurements until Fannie Farmer published her famous cookbook in 1896, when Anne was thirty years old; wood-stove ovens could not be adjusted as scientifically as today's ovens and depended on the cook's experience to add just the right amount of fuel at the right time to arrive at the correct temperature.

Anne eventually mastered the art of cake-baking, although she did have to learn the hard way to make sure of her ingredients – anodyne liniment adds *quite* a different flavour to cake than vanilla! Diana was especially fond of Anne's chocolate cake, and a new neighbour, Mr. J.H. Harrison, was the lucky recipient of a "nut cake…iced with pink icing and adorned with walnuts," which Anne took to him as a peace offering when her cow ruined his grain field.

Angel cake, 36-egg pound cake, buttercup cake and gold-and-silver cakes are also mentioned in the Anne books. Recipes for most of these cakes can be found in many cookbooks, although you might not find the 36-egg pound cake – it was a closely guarded Pringle family secret. Buttercup cake was most likely a very rich yellow cake; Susan Baker's "luxuriant" gold and silver cake was a combination of white and yellow cake, with the two different batters carefully swirled together to create a marble effect or assembled in two layers and iced with fluffy white frosting.

GINGERBREAD

"Meanwhile," said Susan…"here is your gingerbread and whipped cream, Jem dear." Gingerbread and whipped cream was Jem's favourite dessert. But tonight it had no charm to soothe his stormy soul. (ANNE OF INGLESIDE, IV)

Gingerbread has always been a popular dessert. It is easy to make and is especially tempting on crisp autumn afternoons. Molasses will produce a dark, rich gingerbread; dark corn syrup or cane syrup will result in a lighter cake.

¼ cup	butter	50 mL
1 ½ cups	all-purpose flour	375 mL
¼ cup	granulated sugar	50 mL
1 tsp	baking powder	5 mL
¼ tsp	baking soda	1 mL
¼ tsp	salt	1 mL
¼ tsp	ground cloves	1 mL
1 to 2 tsp	ground ginger	5 to 10 mL
1 tsp	ground cinnamon	5 mL
1	egg, beaten	1
½ cup	milk or buttermilk	125 mL
½ cup	molasses	125 mL

1 Preheat your oven to 350 F (180 C).

2 Put the butter in a 9-inch (23-cm) round cake pan and place it in the oven for a few minutes, until the butter melts.

3 Meanwhile, combine the flour, sugar, baking powder, baking soda, salt, cloves, ginger and cinnamon in a bowl.

4 In a separate bowl, combine the egg, milk, molasses and melted butter. Stir this mixture into the dry ingredients.

5 Pour the batter into the cake pan and bake for 30 to 40 minutes, or until a knife or toothpick inserted into the centre of the cake comes out clean.

6 To serve, cut the gingerbread into wedges and serve warm with sweetened whipped cream, or let the cake cool and dust it with sifted icing sugar. To make a pretty pattern, place a paper doily on top of the gingerbread and sift icing sugar over the top. Remove the doily very carefully, and you will have an elegant lacy design on top of the cake!

SWEETENED WHIPPED CREAM

1 cup	whipping cream	250 mL
2 tbsp	granulated sugar	25 mL
1/4 tsp	vanilla or lemon extract	1 mL

1 Pour the cream into a chilled mixing bowl. Beat the cream, slowly at first, then more rapidly, until it begins to thicken. Sprinkle the sugar in gradually and continue beating until peaks begin to form. (Don't beat the cream too long, or it will turn into butter.) Stir in the vanilla or lemon extract. Chill the whipped cream until ready to serve.

ORANGE COCONUT FROSTING

"An orange-frosted cake with coconut" was one of the four cakes Susan Baker made for Aunt Mary Maria's surprise birthday party at Ingleside.

This recipe will make enough frosting for a single-layer sponge cake.

3 tbsp	butter, at room temperature	45 mL
1 1/2 cups	sifted icing sugar	375 mL
2 tsp	grated orange rind	10 mL
1 tbsp	orange juice	15 mL
1/2 cup	grated coconut	125 mL

1 In a bowl, beat the butter until it is fluffy. Add the sugar about 1/2 cup (125 mL) at a time, mixing it thoroughly with the butter. Mix in the orange rind and orange juice.

2 Frost the cooled cake by first spreading a thin layer of frosting on the sides and top of the cake layer. This will seal in any extra crumbs. Then spread the rest of the frosting over the entire cake. Sprinkle coconut over the top and sides of the cake.

SPONGE CAKE

*"Then just let's sit comfily down and eat
everything," said Miss Lavendar happily.
"…It is so fortunate that I made the sponge
cake…"* (ANNE OF AVONLEA, XXI)

This sponge cake recipe is easier than
most because it does not require the
egg whites to be beaten separately before
being folded into the batter. The cake can
be served plain, dusted with icing sugar,
or frosted. It also makes a wonderful base
for strawberry shortcake, one of Gilbert's
favourite desserts.

1 cup	sifted all-purpose flour	250 mL
1 tsp	baking powder	5 mL
1/4 tsp	salt	1 mL
1/2 cup	milk	125 mL
2 tbsp	butter	25 mL
2	eggs	2
1 cup	granulated sugar	250 mL
1 tsp	vanilla	5 mL

1 Preheat your oven to 350 F (180 C).
Grease and flour a 9- or 10-inch (23-
or 25-cm) round cake pan.

2 In a bowl or on a sheet of waxed paper,
sift the flour, baking powder and salt.

3 In a small saucepan, heat the milk and
butter until the butter melts. Keep the
mixture warm until you are ready to add it
to the batter.

4 In a large bowl, beat the eggs until
they are thick and lemon-coloured.
(If you are using an electric mixer, this
should take about three minutes.) Add
the sugar a little at a time while contin-
uing to beat the eggs.

5 With a wooden spoon, stir in the
dry ingredients just until everything
is blended together.

6 Add the warm milk and butter, and
the vanilla. Stir them into the batter.

7 Turn the batter into the pan and bake
for 25 to 30 minutes, or until the cake
springs back when you touch the top of it.

8 Leaving the cake in the pan, set it on
a rack and let it cool completely.

9 Run a sharp knife around the sides of
the cake to loosen it from the pan.
Place a cake rack on top of the cake,
then turn the cake and rack upside down.
Lift off the pan and brush away any loose
crumbs from the side of the cake. Place
a plate on the bottom of the cake and
turn the plate, cake and rack right side up.
Remove the rack. Now the cake can be
sliced and served as is, dusted with icing
sugar, frosted or topped with berries and
whipped cream.

Makes one cake

Other Desserts

Besides cakes and pies, there are other desserts mentioned in the Anne books. Plum puddings were traditionally served at Christmas time, as they are today in many households. Queen pudding was Walter Blythe's favourite dessert (a baked custard made of breadcrumbs, sugar, milk and egg yolks, spread with jam and topped with meringue); and Susan Baker once made a "glorious 'orange shuffle'" to celebrate Anne's recovery from a serious illness (the "shuffle" was probably an orange soufflé, given a new pronunciation by the Blythe children).

Other desserts to consider for your tea party are plum puffs or fresh fruit. Instead of the strawberries we have suggested, you can serve a platter of assorted fruits – peaches, apples, oranges, melons or bananas. Wash the fruits well and slice them. Sprinkle the peach, apple and banana slices with orange or lemon juice to keep them from darkening. Arrange the slices of fruit on a platter and serve.

STRAWBERRIES AND CREAM

"Early strawberries for tea!" exclaimed Miss Lavendar…"Girls, when you come back with your strawberries we'll have tea out here under the silver poplar. I'll have it all ready for you with home-grown cream."

(ANNE OF AVONLEA, XXVII)

The wild strawberries Anne and Charlotta the Fourth picked in Mr. Kimball's pasture were tinier and sweeter than the ones we find in today's markets, but fresh strawberries are still a welcome treat on the tea table.

Choose ripe, unblemished berries, and allow at least $\frac{1}{2}$ cup (125 mL) per guest. Remove the hulls, wash the berries well and drain them in a colander. Serve the berries in small bowls accompanied by a pitcher of whipping cream to pour over them, or a bowlful of sweetened whipped cream (page 78) to spoon on top.

Another way to serve strawberries for tea is to put a cupful or so of sifted icing sugar in a small bowl, set it in the middle of a platter and surround it with unhulled washed berries. Your guests can hold the berries by their stems, dip them into the sugar, and eat them with their fingers!

PLUM PUFFS

The cheerful supper table, with the twins' bright faces, and Marilla's matchless plum puffs…of which Davy ate four…did "hearten her up" considerably…. (ANNE OF AVONLEA, XII)

Both Marilla and Susan Baker made fruit "puffs" on occasion, and they would make an unusual and delicious addition to your tea party menu.

Plums are mentioned often in the Anne books, probably because they were so plentiful and versatile. There were both cultivated plums and wild plums, which could be preserved whole or made into jam. Plum jam was a particular favourite of Davy Keith, who "had no sorrows that plum jam could not cure." Davy also considered plum cake a delicacy, but in that instance the "plums" were actually raisins, sometimes called plums in those days. (The "plums" in Christmas plum puddings are also raisins.)

Your tea party guests probably don't need heartening up as Anne did after her "Jonah day" at school, but they will be delighted with these puffs just the same.

½ cup	water	125 mL
3 tbsp	butter	45 mL
½ cup	all-purpose flour	125 mL
1 tsp	granulated sugar	5 mL
2	eggs	2
½ cup	plum jam	125 mL
½ cup	cream cheese or whipped cream	125 mL
	Sifted icing sugar	

1 Preheat your oven to 425 F (220 C). Grease a baking sheet lightly.

2 In a large saucepan, heat the water and butter until boiling. When the butter has melted, turn the heat to low, add the flour and sugar all at once and mix them in thoroughly (a wooden spoon seems to work best for this). Continue to beat the mixture over low heat until it leaves the sides of the pan, about 1 minute.

3 Remove the pan from the heat. Add one egg and beat the mixture until it is smooth. Add the second egg and beat again until smooth.

4 Drop the dough by teaspoonfuls onto the baking sheet, about 2 inches (5 cm) apart; they should be about 1 inch (2.5 cm) around. (The puffs will double in size as they bake.) Bake for 15 to 20 minutes, or until they are golden-brown.

5 Take the puffs out of the oven and turn the heat off. Close the oven door. With a toothpick or thin skewer, poke a tiny hole or two in each puff to let the steam out. Return the puffs to the turned-off but warm oven for about 5 more minutes to ensure that the insides are done. Remove the puffs from the oven and cool them on a rack.

6 When cool, gently split the puffs in half and fill each one with a spoonful of jam and a dab of cream cheese or whipped cream. When all the puffs are filled, arrange them on a platter and sift icing sugar over the top.

Makes 2 to 3 dozen small puffs

Extra Touches

If you have some of Anne's favourite flowers in your garden or windowbox, why not use a few of them to decorate your table and platters? Fresh, sugared or candied flowers can be used as garnishes for your tea-time treats. Just make sure the plants have not been treated with pesticides or other chemicals and rinse them well several times.

Fresh flowers, whether a single rose or a nosegay of mixed flowers, can decorate a tray of sandwiches or cookies. You could also place a tiny edible flower such as a violet or rosebud or rose petals on top of each frosted cookie or tiny cake. And don't overlook the possibilities of using fresh leaves – tendrils of ivy or little fronds of ferns encircling a cake, for example, are irresistible.

Anne enjoyed scattering ferns and flowers on the tablecloth for special occasions. She might place a rose at each person's place, and even for an everyday sort of tea, she would try to have a vase of fresh flowers on the table.

A cluster of sugared flowers arranged on top of a cake looks lovely, and the flowers can be prepared a few hours in advance. To sugar flowers, dip each one gently into foamy beaten egg white, drain off the excess, then sprinkle the flowers with granulated sugar. Place on waxed paper to dry thoroughly.

Candied violets look elegant sprinkled on a cake or pie, or they can be used singly on individual tarts or cakes (use only wild violets, preferably the *Viola odorata* variety). To candy flowers, in a saucepan, bring to a boil ½ cup (125 mL) granulated sugar and 2 tbsp (25 mL) water. Boil the mixture, stirring occasionally, until it forms a light syrup. Cool.

Dip each flower into the syrup, shaking off the excess before laying it on waxed paper to dry. With a toothpick, straighten out the petals that may have become folded. Sprinkle the flowers lightly with granulated sugar, if desired. When the flowers are thoroughly dry, store them carefully in a tin until ready to use.

* * *

They say all good things must come to an end. We hope you and your friends have had a wonderful Anne tea party. Please don't forget to wash all the dishes and put away any leftover treats. Then you can start thinking about what to serve at your *next* tea party!

CHAPTER 6

Busy Hands

"Miss Cornelia held that the woman whose hands were employed always had the advantage over the woman whose hands were not."

(RAINBOW VALLEY, 11)

The women and girls in the Anne books were nearly always busy with some kind of domestic activity, whether household duties, farm chores, gardening or making something to wear or use in the home. They rarely sat still – almost every hour of the day and evening was devoted to doing something useful. Whenever they went calling on their friends and neighbours, they usually took along their knitting or crocheting projects to work on while they chatted.

Girls were expected to do a bit of handwork each day. Anne's first project at Green Gables was a red and white diamond-patterned patchwork piece – not her favourite activity! "There's no scope for imagination in patchwork," she once said. "It's just one little seam after another and you never seem to be getting anywhere."

Patchwork quilts, however, were born of necessity. Because cloth was scarce, every scrap was saved, and many of these scraps were sewn together to form large pieces of cloth, usually to serve as blankets. (One of Mrs. Lynde's prize quilts contained five thousand pieces!) In some communities it was the custom for girls to stitch up to twenty patchwork quilts before they were sixteen, in order to have an adequate supply for their homes when they married.

When scraps of clothing weren't being recycled into patchwork, they were often turned into braided rugs. Since skirts and coats were long and full, quite a lot of yardage was available. Long strips of fabric were braided, coiled into a flat shape, and then sewn together.

Most of the handwork was of a practical nature – the women of Anne's day made many of their home furnishings and most of their family's clothing. In the Anne books, Mrs. Rachel Lynde's specialty was knitted cotton-warp quilts; Marilla made braided rugs; and there were always stockings to knit, skirts to hem and mending to finish.

In addition to the necessary handwork, there was also ornamental handwork. Anne's bosom friend Diana crocheted lace doilies for her hope chest; Anne's college friend Philippa Gordon loved embroidery; and Susan Baker, Anne's housekeeper at Ingleside, was proud of the crocheted lace with which she trimmed her aprons. Miss Lavendar Lewis, who lived at the little stone cottage called Echo Lodge, preserved rose petals and other flowers to add a delicate and delightful scent to the rooms.

You can bring a touch of Anne's world into your home, too, with these simple craft projects.

MISS LAVENDAR'S ROSE BOWL

Echo Lodge, which had been closed ever since Miss Lavendar's wedding, was briefly thrown open to wind and sunshine once more, and firelight glimmered again in the little rooms. The perfume of Miss Lavendar's rose bowl still filled the air. (ANNE OF THE ISLAND, VII)

One of the simplest yet most delightful ways to begin adding Anne touches to your home is to start a rose bowl (also called potpourri) similar to the one Miss Lavendar had at Echo Lodge. Potpourri is a wonderful way to capture the fragrance of summer flowers and herbs to savour all winter long.

The traditional basis of scented potpourri is dried rose petals, but you can also use other scented and unscented flowers such as lavender, peonies, marigolds, lilacs, violets, tulips, petunias, geraniums, carnations, hosta lilies and statice.

Scented leaves or herbs could include scented geranium, different kinds of mint, rose or lavender leaves, lemon verbena, thyme, rosemary, and blackberry or raspberry leaves.

Suitable spices would be bay leaves, cinnamon, whole cloves and allspice, nutmeg, cardamom, caraway, ginger, anise or fennel seed. (Avoid adding powdered spices to potpourri – they will make the potpourri and its container look dusty and discoloured.) Lemon or orange peel can be sliced into thin strips and dried as well. And finely chopped or shredded fragrant woods such as sandalwood, cedar or eucalyptus can add scent as well as texture.

Fixatives, most commonly orris root (which itself has a slightly sweet fragrance), are used to help retain the scents of the flowers and herbs. While ladies in Anne's day ground their own orris root from irises (*Iris florentina* or *Iris pallida*), today it is conveniently available in many craft shops. Use 2 to 4 tablespoons (25 to 50 mL) per gallon (4 L) of potpourri. (P.S. Susan Baker, the housekeeper at Ingleside, boiled sheets in orris root to give them a pleasant scent.)

Fragrant oils for scenting potpourri can be found in craft shops (though Anne and Miss Lavendar would have purchased them at a pharmacy). There are dozens of fragrances to choose from – rose, gardenia, lavender, geranium, herbal and many others. A drop or two of one oil (or perhaps even a mixture) can be added to the fixative to enhance or create a scent for your potpourri – it's fun to experiment to see which scents suit your fancy. Try a drop each of rose and lavender oils, or a combination of honeysuckle and lilac.

HOW TO MAKE POTPOURRI

Concocting potpourri is not an exact science; you simply add and mix your choice of ingredients in the amounts that please you.

Pick flowers in the morning, after the dew has evaporated, but before the heat of the sun has extracted too much of their scent. Roses should be picked between the bud stage and full opening; other flowers can be picked just as they are beginning to open.

Cut the flower heads from their stems, leaving as little stem on as possible. Lay the flower heads in a single layer on screens or newspaper in a warm airy place out of direct sunlight. The flowers will shrink slightly while drying; the petals will be completely dry in about a week (they should feel crisp to the touch).

For potpourri in its simplest form, simply place the flowers in decorative bowls or baskets for display, leaving the dried flower heads whole or separating them into petals. However, if you like, you can add more ingredients to the potpourri.

To every 4 cups (1 L) dried flower heads and petals, add as little as a tablespoon or as much as a cup (15 to 250 mL) scented leaves, herbs and slivered peels that have been dried in the same way the flowers were dried. You can also add 1 tbsp (15 mL) cloves, allspice or chopped cinnamon stick to every 4 cups (1 L) potpourri, or perhaps a sprinkling or two of thyme.

A tablespoonful (15 mL) of chopped orris root per 4 cups (1 L) dried materials will help preserve the scents. A drop or two of fragrant oil can be added to intensify and enhance the fragrance of your potpourri (the scent can easily become too strong, so be sparing in the use of the oils). Cure the scented potpourri by storing it in a large covered jar or tightly closed plastic bag for two to three weeks. Display it in an attractive bowl or other container.

If the scent begins to fade after a while, it can be revived by stirring the mixture or by adding another drop or two of fragrant oil.

FRAGRANT SACHETS

The women of Anne's day used potpourri not only as a decorative accent or room freshener; they also used it to scent clothing in closets and drawers, to stuff pillows and cushions, and even to keep moths and other pests away from stored linen (lavender, southernwood, mint, rosemary, thyme, sage and tansy are said to be especially good for this purpose).

Try making these simple sachets. Tuck one among your lingerie, handkerchiefs, linens and sweaters, or place a sachet in your luggage to keep it from developing a musty odour. And a little basket filled with several plump sachets makes a delightful hostess gift!

1 Cut a 6-inch (15-cm) square of lightweight but tightly woven material such as cotton batiste, organdy, dotted Swiss or satin (try using fabric with a small floral print). Hem the edges, or trim them with pinking shears.

2 Place 1 to 2 tsp (5 to 10 mL) dried potpourri in the centre of the square.

3 Gather the material around the potpourri to form a pouch and tie tightly with ribbon. Hang the sachet on a hanger in your closet, or on a doorknob, or put it among clothes in a drawer.

POTPOURRI PILLOWS

For a delicately scented room or to induce a restful sleep, stitch up a potpourri pillow. (Anne made one and filled it with fir needles to use for her naps – she was sure it would help her dream that she was a dryad or wood nymph!)

1 Cut two pieces of tightly woven fabric. You can make the pillow any size you like, but an 8-inch (20-cm) square is a manageable size.

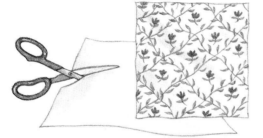

2 With the right sides of the material together, machine-stitch around all four sides, leaving a ⅝-inch (15-mm) seam allowance. Leave a 2-inch (5-cm) opening in one side. Turn the pillow case inside out.

3 Loosely fill the pillow case with potpourri and stitch the opening closed.

4 Make a pillow cover from a decorative fabric of your choice, cut the same size as the cotton pieces for the pillow. This time leave a ½-inch (13-mm) seam allowance, and stitch the pillow closed on three sides. Press the seams open, turn the cover inside out and slip the potpourri pillow into the cover. Then stitch the fourth side closed. If you like, you can add a lace or ribbon trim. Tuck the pillow under your own pillow at night – for a relaxing sleep and sweet dreams!

BIB APRON

Presently Marilla came briskly in with some of Anne's freshly ironed school aprons.

(ANNE OF GREEN GABLES, XX)

The apron Anne wore over her school dresses was actually more of a sleeveless "smock" that covered most of the front and back of the dress. Here are instructions for making a simpler, more decorative apron to wear over your dresses or when you are helping in the kitchen. You can make the apron in any colour, or in a printed fabric, but white eyelet is always pretty.

You will need ⅝ yard (50 cm) of 45-inch (115-cm) wide lightweight cotton material such as batiste, calico, eyelet or dotted Swiss; 3 yards (3 m) of ¾-inch or 1-inch (20-or 25-mm) grosgrain or satin ribbon; and matching thread.

1 Spread the fabric out flat. Cut 10 inches (25 cm) off one side of the fabric (parallel to the selvage edges) so that you have two pieces of fabric – one will be 35 inches (87.5 cm) wide and one will be 10 inches (25 cm) wide.

2 From the 10-inch (25-cm) piece, cut a piece 18 inches (45 cm) long. (You can use the leftover material for potpourri sachets – see page 89.) Fold this piece in half with the wrong sides together so that you have a doubled piece of fabric, 10 by 9 inches (25 by 22.5 cm). Press and set aside. (This will be the top or bib part of the apron.)

3 Finish the sides of the remaining 35-inch (87.5-cm) piece of material by turning over the short sides about ¼ inch (5 mm). Press the folded edges down. Turn them over again about ½-inch (13-mm) and stitch down.

4 To hem the bottom edge, turn up the material ¼ inch (5 mm) and press. Turn up again for a 2-inch (5-cm) hem; press and stitch in place.

5 Turn the top edge over ½ inch (13 mm) with the right sides together. Press. Sew a row of long basting stitches ½ inch (13 mm) from the top edge of the material, all the way across the skirt.

6 Gently pull the basting thread to gather the material until it is 16 to 20 inches (40 to 50 cm) wide – wide enough to cover your front and go around the sides a bit. Stitch the gathers in place ⅜ inch (10 mm) from the edge. Set the skirt aside while you make the bib.

7 To make the bib, fold the double thickness up ¼ inch (5 mm) on both sides. Press.

8 Pin one end of the ribbon to the front bottom corner of the bib, covering the turned-up side edge. The outer edge of the ribbon should lie along the outer edge of the bib. Pin the ribbon along the side of the bib to hold it in place. Make a loop large enough to slip over your head (but not so large that the bib will be too loose) and then run the ribbon down the other side of the bib, outer edges even, to the bottom corner, and pin in place. Now try on the bib to see if the neck loop is the right size; make any necessary adjustments and cut off the excess ribbon.

9 Stitch the ribbon into place on both sides, first along the outer edge, then across the top where the bib ends, then down the inner edge.

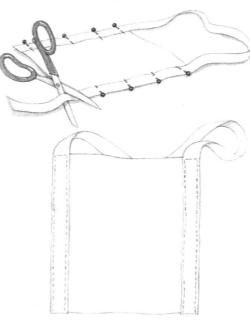

10 To join the bib and skirt, find the centre of both pieces by folding each in half lengthwise. Mark each centre on the raw edge with a pin.

11 Spread the skirt right side up on a flat surface. Place the bib right side up on the skirt. The raw edge of the bib should overlap the raw edge of the skirt by ½ inch (13 mm), and the centre pins should match. Pin the bib to the skirt.

12 Fold the remaining piece of ribbon in half and mark the centre point with a pin. Pin the ribbon along the right side of the apron, just covering the gathered seam with the bottom edge of the ribbon, and matching the centre points. You should have about 20 inches (50 cm) extra ribbon on each side for the ties. Stitch the ribbon in place along the bottom and top edges. (The top edge of the ribbon should come just above the top edge of the skirt.)

If you want to add a bit of lace edging (you can use the crocheted edging on page 106 or buy ready-made lace trim at a fabric store), hand-sew the edging along the top edge of the bib. Or stitch a length of lace or ready-made ruffle to the bottom edge of the apron skirt.

There are many other ways you can decorate your apron – rows of embroidery (Anne liked feather-stitching) or tiny embroidered flowers (Anne's college friend, Philippa Gordon, embroidered tiny rosebuds on one of Anne's dresses, and the result was "the envy of every Redmond girl"!); you could put rows of tiny tucks at the apron hemline or at the top of the bib, or you could stitch some ribbon bows with long streamers to the top two corners of the bib or at the waist. Perhaps you would even like to sew five or six of the buttons from your button collection (see next page) to the apron's waistband!

BUTTON COLLECTING

What gave Nan the idea that God might be induced to grant her petitions by promises of good behaviour or displays of fortitude would be hard to say....

...But when she asked Him to send her a special button for her button-string... collecting buttons had broken out every-where among the Glen small girls like the measles...the button came the very next day, Susan having found one on an old dress in the attic. A beautiful red button set with tiny diamonds, or what Nan believed to be dia-monds. She was the envied of all because of that elegant button... (ANNE OF INGLESIDE, XXV)

Many girls in the late 1880s and early 1900s collected buttons to add to their "charm strings," as they were sometimes called. Some collected the buttons simply because they enjoyed the wide variety of materials, colours, shapes and designs. Others had a specific goal in mind – they tried to collect one thousand buttons on their string, for they believed they would then meet the person they would marry.

Every family had its button box, passed down through the generations, because buttons were never thrown away. They were saved to be used again and again. Imagine the happy hours Anne must have spent browsing through Marilla's button box, and then later watching her own

girls rummage in the Ingleside button box looking for "treasure." Many of the buttons must have stirred memories of the garments they had adorned and the occasions on which they had been worn.

Serious button collecting became pop-ular in the 1920s and 1930s, as people be-gan to realize that the carefully crafted handmade buttons of previous centuries were giving way to mass-produced ones. Both methods and materials changed quickly as the manufacture of buttons in-creased.

Until the nineteenth century, buttons were considered an extravagance, used chiefly as ornaments rather than as fas-teners for clothing. They were made indi-vidually, carved from ivory, shells, wood, bone or horn, or moulded from various metals such as gold, silver, brass, bronze, pewter or copper. Many buttons were set with precious or semi-precious stones. Porcelain, glass, enamelwork and pearl began to be used for buttons in the eigh-teenth and nineteenth centuries.

The range of button designs is enor-mous, from plain to geometric to pictorial. Pictures of plants, animals, insects, faces, landscapes, buildings, sports equipment, military insignia and coats of arms are among the hundreds of themes illustrated on buttons. Carving, etching, painting, gilding, embossing, pressing, die-casting and mosaic work are some of the many ways designs are executed

There are many people who collect buttons today. Some look for buttons made of certain materials; others collect buttons that portray a certain subject. Still others search for buttons made during a specific period of history. All collectors are aware of the button as a form of art in miniature and as a tiny record of history.

If you would like to start a button string as Nan and her friends did, you will need a sturdy piece of thread, such as buttonhole twist, on which to string the buttons. See if there is a family button box from which you may select buttons. You might then ask friends and neighbours if they have buttons to donate to your collection. Fabric stores stock a wide variety of buttons that you may want to buy especially for your button string. If some of your friends collect buttons, too, have a button party and trade buttons with each other. For refreshment, serve tea and cookies (see Chapter 5).

The buttons you collect do not have to be antique or expensive. Perhaps there are certain colours or shapes or themes you want to collect, or you may simply want to collect a wide variety of buttons. It will be easier to display buttons with "shanks" (little loops on the backs used for attaching them to garments).

To keep the buttons from slipping off, tie a small button at one end of the string and keep the ends of the string tied securely except when you are adding new buttons or rearranging your collection. You may want to wear your button string as a necklace or belt, or hang it from a hook in your room.

As you continue to learn more about button collecting, you may find yourself agreeing with Charles Dickens, who wrote about buttons in *Household Words* in the 1800s: "There is surely something charming in seeing the smallest thing done so thoroughly, as if to remind the careless that whatever is worth doing is worth doing well."

ANNE'S FLOWERED HAT

Her hat was a little, flat, glossy, new sailor, the extreme plainness of which had likewise much disappointed Anne, who had permitted herself secret visions of ribbon and flowers. The latter, however, were supplied before Anne reached the main road, for being confronted halfway down the lane with a golden frenzy of wind-stirred buttercups and a glory of wild roses, Anne promptly and liberally garlanded her hat with a heavy wreath of them. (ANNE OF GREEN GABLES, XI)

To make your own version of Anne's notorious flower-garlanded hat, you will need a plain straw hat, 2 ½ yards (2.5 m) of 1 ½-inch (4-cm) dark-green grosgrain or satin ribbon, six stems of yellow buttercup-type silk flowers, and four stems of small pink silk roses. (Should you wish to use other colours or types of flowers, we are quite sure Anne would approve!) You will also need fine floral wire, a small wire cutter, green florist's tape, a heavy-duty needle, strong green thread and scissors.

1 Cut a piece of wire about 3 inches (7.5 cm) longer than the circumference of the hat's crown. Form the wire into a ring the size and shape of the crown; twist the ends together and clip off the extra wire. Attach bunches of buttercups and roses alternately to the outside of the wire ring with florist's tape or wire; if the flower stems are long, clip off the excess. Set aside.

2 Encircle the crown of the hat once with ribbon, overlapping the ends by about ½ inch (13 mm) at the back of the hat. Trim and stitch the ends together with matching thread.

3 Stitch the ribbon in several places around the crown to hold the ribbon in place.

4 Place the ring of flowers over the crown of the hat. Stitch the ring to the hat in several places to secure it. Adjust the flowers so that the wire and tape do not show.

5 Cut two 16-inch (40-cm) pieces of ribbon for streamers; stitch them together at one end and attach to the crown ribbon at the back of the hat. Cut the ends of the streamers on the diagonal or in a V-shape.

The hat can be worn or hung on the wall as a decoration. You can also make miniature versions – doll-sized straw hats can sometimes be found in craft shops or sewing-notions stores. Adjust the width and length of the ribbon and the size and number of flowers to complement the size of the hat. These small hats can be used as wall decorations or even Christmas tree ornaments.

BABY BONNET

The babies of Anne's era wore little caps or bonnets nearly all the time – even in their cribs!

To make a little bonnet or christening cap such as the one here, you will need a 13-inch (32-cm) square white handkerchief that has a border of lace at least 1 inch (25 mm) wide, 24 inches (60 cm) of ¼-inch (5-mm) white satin ribbon, a needle and white thread.

1 Place the handkerchief right side down on a flat surface.

2 Fold the left side of the handkerchief over about 2 ½ inches (6 cm). Fold the right side of the handkerchief over about 4 inches (10 cm). The lace edges of the two folded sides should almost meet. Press.

3 With a needle and thread, make ½-inch (13-mm) basting stitches about ½ inch (13 mm) from the folded edge, leaving an extra inch or two of thread at each end. Remove the needle.

4 Now shape the bonnet by gently pulling the two ends of the basting stitches to gather the basted edge. This will form the back of the bonnet. Tie the ends of the basting threads together firmly and snip off the extra thread.

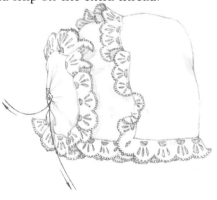

5 Cut the ribbon into two 12-inch (30-cm) lengths. Fold one end of each length about ½ inch (13 mm) from the end. Stitch each folded end about ½ inch (13 mm) from each of the two front corners of the bonnet. Remove the pins.

Be sure to save the bonnet, for it has another use in the baby's future. When the baby grows up and is to be married, the basting threads and ribbon ties can be removed, and the resulting handkerchief can be carried at the wedding. (If the baby who wears the bonnet is a boy, he can give it to his bride for her to carry at their wedding!)

PS If you cannot find a ready-made handkerchief the right size for this project, it is very easy to make one yourself. You will need an 11-inch (28-cm) square of finely woven lightweight material such as batiste, and 1½ yards (1.5 metres) of 1-inch (25-mm) lace. (If you want to use wider lace, the square of material can be smaller.

1 Put the tiniest hem possible on the square of material by turning the edges of the material under about 1/16 inch (1 mm); press them down. Turn these edges under again about 1/16 inch (1 mm) and stitch them with very fine stitches.

2 Cut the lace into four pieces to fit the sides of the handkerchief. The corners of the lace should be cut at an angle, as shown.

3 Pin the lace to the handkerchief hem. Make sure it is straight and smooth. The angled corners of the lace should meet and overlap just enough to allow them to be stitched together. Stitch the lace to the hem with tiny stitches; then stitch the corners of the lace together.

Pressing Flowers

"I feel as if I had opened a book and found roses of yesterday, sweet and beloved, between its leaves." (ANNE OF THE ISLAND, XXI)

The sentimental age of the Victorians (as people who lived during the reign of Queen Victoria were called) gave rise to many customs that reflected their interest in nostalgia and remembrance. Placing a rose or other flower between the pages of a book preserved the flower and, thus, the memory of the sweet occasion it represented. When a young lady received a nosegay or bouquet for a special party, she would press at least one of the flowers as a keepsake of the evening. Brides pressed flowers from their bridal bouquets. Even young men were not immune to sentiment in those days – Diana happened to notice a certain gentleman discreetly retrieve a rose of Anne's one evening. No doubt Gilbert pressed that rose, perhaps in a book of poetry, and kept it.

Pressing flowers need not be limited to souvenirs of bygone moments. They can be made into very attractive arrangements for pictures, greeting cards, bookmarks, place cards or other decorative objects.

Place the flowers carefully between the pages of a heavy book such as an outdated telephone book or encyclopedia volume. Fairly flat flowers such as violets, pansies, buttercups and asters are the easiest to begin with.

Place the flowers face down, as close to the binding side of the page as possible. With your fingertip, press down on the backs of the flowers at their centres; this will help spread the petals out in their natural position. Slowly roll the pages of the book down on top of the flowers to close the book and hold the flowers in place. With both hands, press down on the top of the closed book to firmly flatten the flowers inside. If you have a number of flowers, repeat this process in the same book, leaving a few pages between each group of flowers. Set another heavy book or brick on top of the book to weight it down further.

Leave the flowers in place for a week or so. (You may want to check them after the first day to see if the petals need to be rearranged; if so, use your fingertip or a toothpick to do this.) When you are ready to arrange the flowers, remove them from the book and spread them on a piece of white paper. Choose the flowers you want to use for your project and decide on the arrangement. Then with tiny dots of glue (white glue is ideal) on the backs of the petals, stems and leaves, attach the flowers to the card or paper they will adorn. You can paint on extra touches such as tendrils, leaves, berries and flowerbuds if you like.

You needn't limit your pressings to flowers. Leaves from clover, ivy, ferns, herbs and some evergreens press well. Experiment with different flowers and leaves at different seasons.

PRESSED FLOWER PICTURE

You will need a frame with a background card or paper. You can find ready-made frames, complete with glass and backs, in many craft shops and variety stores. You will also need glue and perhaps some coloured pencils or paints to add extra details.

1 Arrange your pressed flowers on the background card. When you are satisfied with the arrangement, glue the flowers in place.

2 When the glue has set, put the picture in the frame. Place the back of the frame on and your picture will be ready to hang on a wall, set on a table, or be given as a very personal gift.

PRESSED FLOWER PLACE CARD

Are you having friends over for lunch or tea? Place cards will add a delightful touch to the table. They tell each guest where she is to sit; and, after the party, she can take her place card home as a souvenir.

For each card, you will need a piece of heavy paper or card stock about 2 by 3 inches (5 by 7.5 cm), pressed flowers and glue.

1 Fold the card in half so that it measures about 1 by 3 inches (2.5 by 7.5 cm).

2 Arrange one or two small pressed flowers on one end of the front of the card. Glue them in place. Draw or paint on extra leaves or tendrils if you wish.

3 Write the guest's name beside the flowers.

PRESSED FLOWER BOOKMARK

You will need heavy paper or card stock, pressed flowers, glue, fine net or lace (optional), and about 12 inches (30 cm) of narrow ribbon.

1 Cut a piece of heavy paper or card to the size you wish, perhaps 1 by 5 inches (2.5 by 12 cm).

2 Decide on the arrangement for your flowers and glue them in place. Draw or paint on extra leaves or tendrils if desired.

3 Cut a piece of net or lace the same size as or slightly smaller than the bookmark. Carefully place the net on top of the pressed flowers and glue all four edges of the net to the bookmark. This will help protect the delicate pressed flowers.

4 To cover the raw edges, glue a piece of narrow ribbon around the edges of the bookmark.

5 Punch a hole in the top or bottom of the card and tie a short piece of ribbon onto the card as an extra decoration, if you wish.

PRESSED FLOWER GREETING CARD

You will need a piece of heavy paper, pressed flowers, glue, tissue paper and an envelope.

1 Fold a piece of heavy paper in half; trim it to the size you want your card to be (slightly smaller than your envelope).

2 Decide on your flower arrangement and glue the pressed flowers in place on the front of the card.

3 Write a personal message on the inside of the card and sign your name.

4 For an extra touch, make a notation on the back of the card about the flowers, such as: "This card of pressed violets and ferns (or whatever flowers you have used) was made especially for you by _____ (your name)." You might look up the meanings of the flowers you have used (see pages 124 to 141) and write in this information as well ("Blue violets signify faithfulness; ferns sincerity or fascination.").

5 To help protect the pressed flowers, cut a piece of tissue the same size as the front of the card and place it over the arrangement. Then slip the card and tissue into the envelope and deliver it to a friend. You could also use one of these cards to enclose with a gift.

PRESSED FLOWER SCRAPBOOK

1 Buy or make a booklet of blank pages.

2 Arrange pressed flowers on each page. Write the name of each flower and its meaning beside it or under it (see pages 124 to 141). You might also want to include where you found the flower – in your own garden, along a woodland path, beside a roadway – or any other information. Perhaps the flower came from a special bouquet or corsage that someone special gave you! Be sure to make a note of the occasion and the date.

3 To protect the delicate flowers, you may want to cut pieces of tissue paper to fit over each page.

When you visit a special place, collect a few flowers and leaves to press and arrange as a memento of your visit (ask permission first, of course!). Make sure you note where you found the flowers and the date of your trip.

CROCHETED LACE

"Diana showed me a new fancy crochet stitch her aunt over at Carmody taught her." (ANNE OF GREEN GABLES, XVIII)

Crocheting lace and other items was one of the most popular pastimes for the ladies of Anne's day. It was easy to carry along when going visiting – all that was needed was a crochet hook and a ball of thread. Several inches of lace could be finished in the hour or two spent chatting in the sitting room or on a neighbour's front porch. The lace was used to trim pillowcases, sheets, napkins, linen towels, aprons, petticoats and other clothing and household items.

There are references to crocheted lace throughout the Anne books. Anne's pillows were trimmed with Mrs. Lynde's crocheted lace, and Susan Baker proudly sported "an apron trimmed with crochet lace five inches deep made from Number One Hundred thread" when the Ladies' Aid came to Ingleside for their quilting.

There are hundreds of crochet patterns for lace edgings, from simple to very complicated, that you can find in books, magazines and pamphlets. Included here is a simple crocheted lace edging that will give an Anne touch to an apron, tea towel, pillowcase or handkerchief. If you are crocheting for the first time, ask someone who is experienced with crochet to help you learn the stitches; it is not difficult, but you may need some help in the beginning.

For this picot edging, you'll need fine cotton yarn and a small steel crochet hook, International size 1.5 to 1.25 mm (American size 8 to 10).

Abbreviations

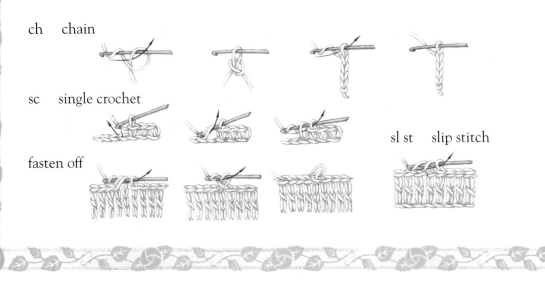

ch   chain

sc   single crochet

sl st   slip stitch

fasten off

1 Make a chain the length required. The number of stitches should be divisible by four.

2 Row 1: 1 sc into 4th ch from hook, 1 sc into each ch to end.

3 Row 2: *6 ch, sl st into 4th ch from hook, 2 ch, skip 2 sc, 1 sc into next sc, repeat from * to end.

4 Fasten off.

5 Wash the trim before attaching it to anything so that if the trim should shrink slightly, it will not alter the shape of the article it is attached to. Press the trim lightly, gently stretching it back into shape if necessary.

6 Beginning at a seam or corner of an article, pin the edging into the desired position. Stitch the edging to the article with thread matching the colour of the edging, using very fine stitches. Backstitch every few inches for added strength.

Helpful Household Hints
from the Anne Books

Had one of the Ladies' Aid organizations in Avonlea, Summerside or Glen St. Mary published a book of helpful household hints from Island residents, here are a few tips that might have been included.

To get rid of warts, rub them with a pebble from the creek; throw the pebble over your left shoulder when the moon is new.
— Ruby Gillis, Avonlea
(ANNE OF GREEN GABLES, XVI)

To have rain tomorrow, kill a toad today.
— Benjie Sloane, Avonlea
(ANNE OF AVONLEA, XI)

A little lemon juice dabbed on freckles will help them disappear.
— Diana Barry, Orchard Slope, Avonlea
(ANNE OF AVONLEA, XVI)

If you get out of bed on the wrong side, things are likely to go wrong the rest of the day. — Milty Boulter, Avonlea
(ANNE OF AVONLEA, XXII)

Do not plant seeds, kill pigs, or cut your hair when the moon is dark.
— Milty Boulter, Avonlea; this hint was also sent in by Davy Keith, Green Gables, Avonlea
(ANNE OF AVONLEA, XXIV)

If there is a diamond-shaped crease in the centre of a fresh sheet, there will be a death in the household. — Mrs. Lincoln MacLean, Windy Poplars, Summerside
(ANNE OF WINDY POPLARS, FIRST YEAR, III)

Wearing black to a wedding will bring the bride bad luck.
— Anne Shirley, Windy Poplars
(ANNE OF WINDY POPLARS, FIRST YEAR, XIII)

*To cure a nosebleed, drop a door-key
down your back.*
— Mrs. James Kennedy, Bonnyview
(ANNE OF WINDY POPLARS, FIRST YEAR, XVI)

*A Christmas with no snow means that there
will be more deaths than usual.*
— Mrs. Rachel Lynde, Avonlea
(ANNE OF WINDY POPLARS, SECOND YEAR, VI)

To be married in May is unlucky.
— Miss Ernestine Bugle, Lowvale
(ANNE OF WINDY POPLARS, SECOND YEAR, VIII)

*A few minutes before midnight on
New Year's Eve, open the door to let the
New Year in.* — Captain James Boyd,
Four Winds Lighthouse
(ANNE'S HOUSE OF DREAMS, XVII)

*For a cold in the head, rub tallow on your
nose before bedtime.*
— Miss Cornelia Bryant,
Four Winds Harbour
(ANNE'S HOUSE OF DREAMS, XXVI)

*Saying a new word twenty-one times will
help you remember it.*
— Jem Blythe, Ingleside, Glen St. Mary
(ANNE OF INGLESIDE, XIX)

*Plant a rowan tree beside the front door
to keep the fairies out.*
— Mrs. Anthony Mitchell, Lower Glen
(ANNE OF INGLESIDE, XXI)

*When you and another person say
the same thing at once, link your fingers
and make a wish.*
— Walter and Di Blythe,
Ingleside, Glen St. Mary
(ANNE OF INGLESIDE, XXVII)

*For a sore throat, make a poultice of red
flannel, turpentine and goose-grease and tie
it around your throat at bedtime.*
— Thomasine Fair, Glen St. Mary
(ANNE OF INGLESIDE, XXXVI)

CHAPTER 7

In Fine Fashion

"It is ever so much easier to be good if your clothes are fashionable. At least, it is easier for me."   (ANNE OF GREEN GABLES, XXIX)

It was not until Anne had been at Green Gables for over a year and a half that she received her very first fashionable dress. Until then, she had to content herself with the "good, sensible, serviceable dresses, without any frills or furbelows about them" that Marilla made for her. Anne had to use her imagination to provide the decorative details she would have loved, such as the lace ruffles, tucks, shirring and puffed sleeves that were so popular at the time.

Once Matthew realized how much pretty clothes meant to Anne, he saw to it that she had as many fashionable dresses and accessories as he could afford. And even Marilla softened her opinion that clothes needed to be merely serviceable; eventually she began to make Anne's dresses in the more elegant fabrics and vivid colours that were characteristic of the period.

In rural areas, wardrobes for girls and women alike were usually limited to one or two "best" dresses worn for church and special occasions; one or two "second-best" dresses worn for visiting or entertaining visitors at home; and a few everyday dresses or skirts and blouses worn for school and housekeeping chores. Several aprons were kept on hand to be worn over the everyday dresses to protect them, since aprons were much easier to wash and iron than the dresses, and were much more economical to make.

Most clothing was made at home or by local dressmakers. Isaac Singer had introduced the first practical home sewing machine in 1856 (ten years before Anne was born) and, though it was expensive, many families invested in one because until then, women had to sew everything by hand – clothing, sheets, pillowcases, towels, curtains and table linens. (Women were also expected to knit sweaters, scarves, socks and stockings, gloves and mittens, and other accessories!) So it is likely that Green Gables was equipped with a sewing machine by the time Anne went to live there in 1877.

Even though the sewing machine made the actual sewing of garments much easier, the paper patterns for cutting out the clothes were almost impossible to use because of the complicated way they were printed – a dozen or more dress patterns (size 36 only) would be printed on a single sheet with the lines for each pattern superimposed on the others! It wasn't until the 1870s that the Butterick family introduced the concept of printing individual patterns in a variety of sizes.

In Anne's day, clothing styles did not change quite as quickly as they do now, especially in the rural areas, probably because the time required to make the elaborately designed dresses was as scarce as the money needed to purchase so many yards of cloth and trimming for each dress. It would take up to thirty yards of cloth to make one of the long, full-skirted dresses of the period, so clothes were worn for years before being replaced.

Laundering the family's clothing was also a major undertaking, since there were no automatic washing machines, clothes dryers or electric steam irons to streamline the process. (Electric irons and washing

*At Green Gables...work was done and duties fulfilled
with regularity....* (ANNE OF GREEN GABLES, XXXVII)

machines did not become common until well after the turn of the century.) Water would have to be carried in from the well and poured into a huge pot on the cookstove to be heated. (Ingleside was the first house Anne lived in that had running water.) Two washtubs, a scrubbing board with ridges, a long stick for stirring and lifting the wet clothes out of the water, a large basket or perforated tub for draining wet clothes, and a rack or clothesline for drying the clothes were the basic items of laundry equipment.

First, delicate items were washed by hand in warm soapy water, before being rinsed. Then white items were scrubbed in hot soapy water and set on the stove to boil for a half hour or so. Coloured fabrics were washed separately in the same manner. After the clothes had been boiled, they were drained and rinsed in a tub of clean water. Sometimes blueing, a substance containing blue or violet dye, would be added to the rinse water to brighten white items and prevent them from yellowing. Then each piece had to be wrung out by hand or put through a wringer to remove the excess water. Many cotton and linen items were dipped in a vat of starch solution; the starch gave body to the fabric and made ironing somewhat easier. In good weather the clothes could be hung outside to dry, but on cold or rainy days, a drying rack was set up in the kitchen near the stove.

Fabrics that could not be washed were dry-cleaned with distilled turpentine and other solvents, which left a strong smell, so the clothes would have to be aired before they could be worn again. Pieces of fresh white bread were often rubbed on delicate silks to remove soil.

The day after the laundry was washed and dried, every piece had to be ironed, for none of the fabrics in those days were the least bit wrinkle-free. Several heavy flatirons were heated on the stove. While one iron was being used, the others were kept on the stove so they could be used when the first one cooled off. There were also specialty irons such as crimpers and fluters for ruffles.

In Anne's day, young girls dressed more simply than adults, especially

Anne...looked at it in reverent silence.... "Look at those sleeves!"
(ANNE OF GREEN GABLES, XXV)

in everyday wear. Their skirts came to about mid-calf and often had several horizontal tucks near the hem so they could be lengthened easily as the girls grew taller. Over their dresses, girls wore aprons or pinafores to keep the dresses clean. Sturdy boots, thick knitted stockings, underdrawers, a camisole and several petticoats completed the basic costume.

When girls dressed for church or social gatherings, they wore dresses similar to the ladies of the day, with "as many tucks and frills and shirrings as…taste permitted." The brown gloria (a soft fabric made of cotton and silk) that Matthew gave Anne for Christmas was just such a dress, with its "dainty frills and shirrings," "little ruffle of filmy lace at the neck" and, the crowning glory, its sleeves with "long elbow cuffs, and above them two beautiful puffs divided by rows of shirring and bows of brown silk ribbon."

It was not considered proper for a girl younger than seventeen to put her hair in a chignon or pompadour or other "adult" styles. Instead, young girls wore their hair in long braids, or held back with a ribbon.

While Anne was teaching at Avonlea school (1882-84), she turned seventeen, old enough to begin wearing long skirts. She would also have begun to wear a corset – an extremely uncomfortable undergarment equipped with boning and lacings so that the waist could be squeezed and shaped into the tiniest dimensions possible.

Skirts with bustles and short trains were very fashionable in those days. The bustle was a basket-like wire frame, a rounded pad, or a cluster of ruffles tied just below the waist to make the skirt stand out in the back. Not until the turn of the century did bustles and corsets give way to a more natural silhouette.

Young ladies were expected to follow other customs with regard to their appearance. They were to be covered from neck to toes, not only for decency's sake but also to help maintain the clear, dewy complexion that was considered such a beauty asset. High collars (sometimes rigidly boned and reaching to the bottom of the ear)

"*When I put on longer skirts I shall feel that I have to live up to them...*"   (ANNE OF GREEN GABLES, XXX)

and long sleeves were worn even in summer. On special occasions a short-sleeved dress might be worn, but elbow-length gloves would still cover the arms. Hats were worn whenever ladies went outside, to prevent the sun from damaging their faces and to keep their hair clean. They also wore gloves to protect their hands so they would stay white and immaculate.

Women did not cut their hair, except perhaps in front for a fringe of curls over the forehead. Instead, long hair was worn in elaborate chignons, pompadours or coils.

Many women in the Victorian years wore elaborate jewellery – bracelets, brooches, "earbobs," rings and necklaces. Garnets and pearls were popular gemstones. Instead of wristwatches, ladies wore smaller versions of the men's pocketwatches, as pendants or pinned to their blouses; the faces of the watches were covered by an engraved lid that could be snapped open.

When a family member died, special mourning jewellery made of black stones called "jet" would be worn, sometimes with a lock of the remembered person's hair incorporated into the design. After a year of mourning, purple and grey jewellery (such as Marilla's amethyst brooch, which contained a braid of her mother's hair) could be worn in addition to black.

There are not many mentions of Anne's jewellery in the Anne books. She had a string of pearl beads that Matthew gave her when she was sixteen, and her engagement ring was a circlet of pearls. Later gifts from Gilbert included a tiny pink enameled heart pendant on a gold chain, and a diamond pendant that he gave her on their fifteenth wedding anniversary. Instead of jewellery, it seems, she often wore flowers pinned to her lapel or at her throat, or in her hair.

After teaching in Avonlea for two years, Anne enrolled in Redmond College in Nova Scotia, where she graduated in 1888. It was the custom for young women to carry a nosegay of flowers at the ceremony; on her graduation day, Anne received two bouquets –

"There is so much in the world for us all if we only have the eyes to see it…" (ANNE OF THE ISLAND, XXXVII)

violets from Roy Gardner and lilies-of-the-valley from Gilbert – and had to choose which one to carry.

Calling cards with one's name engraved on them were used frequently in the Victorian era, especially in the more formal social scene of large towns and cities. The cards would accompany gifts or be used to introduce oneself when paying a social call.

At the dances Anne attended, girls carried "dance cards" or booklets to help them remember which partners had requested dances. The most popular girls would have their cards completely filled with names early in the evening, undoubtedly disappointing any gentleman who had waited too late to ask for a dance. Sometimes a girl might pretend her card was full if she didn't want to dance with a certain person, as Anne did with Gilbert after she heard rumours about his engagement to Christine Stuart!

In September, 1891, Anne and Gilbert "were married in the sunshine of the old orchard, circled by the loving and kindly faces of long-familiar friends." She was "the first bride of Green Gables, slender and shining-eyed, in the mist of her maiden veil, with her arms full of roses."

When babies were about three months old, they began to wear shorter dresses than the extra-long gowns they had worn since they were born; both boys and girls would wear these dresses until they were three or four years old. The shorter dresses came to the child's ankles; the longer gowns extended twenty-four to thirty-six inches beyond the feet! (Anne felt "ready to cry" when Little Jem was put into shorter gowns for the first time, and no doubt felt equally sentimental a year or so later when her second son, Walter, was "shortened.")

"Dear God…help all mothers everywhere. We need so much help, with the little sensitive, loving hearts and minds that look to us for guidance and love and understanding." (ANNE OF INGLESIDE, VI)

"But it will be rompers next…and in no time he will be grown up."

(ANNE'S HOUSE OF DREAMS, XL)

CHAPTER 8

In the Garden

"...I love my garden, and I love working in it. To potter with green, growing things, watching each day to see the dear, new sprouts come up, is like taking a hand in creation, I think. Just now my garden is like faith – the substance of things hoped for...." (ANNE'S HOUSE OF DREAMS, XVIII)

Anne loved flowers and plants of all kinds. Her daydreams were often inspired by the sights, scents and sounds of the trees and flowers around her, and whenever she visited friends, ran errands or went to school, she always chose the routes that led her past her favourite spots – Lover's Lane, Willowmere, Violet Vale and Birch Path – whether they took longer or not!

During the first summer after Anne came to Green Gables, Anne and Diana spent many happy hours in the playhouse they created in a ring of birches that lay between Green Gables and the Barry farm, Orchard Slope. They named the spot Idlewild and furnished it with stones cushioned with moss for sitting on. There in the cool peacefulness, the girls held imaginary tea parties with the bits and pieces of cast-off china they had collected. They would spend

Delphinium
(Lightness; levity)

Lily-of-the-Valley
(Return of happiness)

Adam-and-Eve
(Perfection)

their free time arranging and rearranging the "furniture," picking wildflowers in the meadows and woods, sharing dreams and stories, and inventing games and entertainments along the way.

Even as a child at Green Gables, Anne had a garden plot of her own. And in every place she lived – Patty's Place while she was at college; Windy Poplars while she taught at Summerside; her House of Dreams and Ingleside, where she and Gilbert brought up their family – the gardens were always as important to her as the houses.

The Green Gables garden was probably typical of many household gardens in Anne's era – a combination flower and kitchen garden containing vegetables, herbs and flowers. There were orchards on either side of the house and plenty of fruit trees and shrubs in the surrounding countryside. Most households spent weeks in summer and fall canning fruits and vegetables for use during the winter, since commercially canned goods were not widespread until about 1880.

One of the things Anne loved best about her House of Dreams was its rose garden, planted more than sixty years before she and Gilbert came to it – "a double row of rose-bushes that the little girls who went to the Glen school set out there for the schoolmaster's bride." There were also flowerbeds "full of old-fashioned flowers" such as golden glow, daffodils, marigolds and poppies, and "orange lilies at the gate…held up their imperial cups to be filled with the molten gold of August sunshine." The beds were edged with large white quahog (clam) shells, and adding to the enchantment were a fir grove behind the house, birches and "blue-eyed grasses on the bank of the brook," and a "little rustic seat Gilbert had built."

Just as Anne was planning her garden for what would have been their third spring in the House of Dreams, Gilbert suggested that they move to Ingleside, a larger house in the nearby town of Glen St. Mary. Although the house was much larger, had running water and plenty of closets and pantries, Anne was reluctant to give up her beloved House of Dreams. Gilbert managed to convince her of the suitability of the Ingleside house when he pointed out the charms of the grounds that surrounded it:

"Think of that big lawn with those magnificent old trees; and of that splendid hardwood grove behind it – twelve acres of it. What a play place for our children! There's a fine orchard, too, and you've always admired that high brick wall around the garden with the door in it – you've thought it was so like a story-book garden." (ANNE'S HOUSE OF DREAMS, XL)

As the years went by, Ingleside became very dear to Anne, partly because it offered plenty of scope for her increasing passion for gardening. There were daffodils and tiger lilies bordering the front walk; poppies, hollyhocks and more daffodils grouped by the brick wall; there were beds of roses, peonies, pansies, snapdragons (or "snackdragons," as the Ingleside children called them), chrysanthemums, iris, phlox, dahlias, "June lilies," honeysuckle, sweetpeas and delphiniums. The front veranda had its "curtain of vines," and there was mint by the steps, providing "soundless, invisible benedictions" whenever someone brushed by its scented leaves.

The large Ingleside kitchen garden was surrounded by a sweetbriar hedge, and there was a birdbath in one corner. There were berry bushes nearby, as well as plum, pear and apple trees. The Blythe children had their own little garden in which they grew "crooked little rows of young lettuce" and other easy-to-grow vegetables and flowers, just as Anne had done at Green Gables.

Whether she was making solemn vows with Diana in the "bowery wilderness" of Orchard Slope, or admiring the romantic setting of Miss Lavendar's stone-walled garden at Echo Lodge, gardens always provided Anne with inspiration and comfort. One of the simplest ways to bring Anne's world into your own is to become familiar with the flowers she loved. You will soon notice how every season brings new delights, and you will start to see Anne's favourites everywhere – flowers in your neighbours' gardens, rose gardens in parks, wildflowers along the roadside – even ivy covering brick walls!

Here are a few ideas for getting you started in Anne's most cherished pastime – loving and caring for flowers.

Iris
(Message)

Mint
(Goodness)

Dahlia
(Dignity; elegance)

A Meaningful Anne Bouquet

"These roses are very late – they bloom after all the others have gone – and they hold all the warmth and soul of the summer come to fruition," said Owen, plucking some of the glowing, half-opened buds. *"The rose is the flower of love – the world has acclaimed it so for centuries. The pink roses are love hopeful and expectant – the white roses are love dead or forsaken – but the red roses – ah, Leslie, what are the red roses?"*

"Love triumphant," said Leslie in a low voice.

"Yes – love triumphant and perfect." (ANNE'S HOUSE OF DREAMS, XXXVIII)

In the Victorian era, a silent but eloquent "language" evolved, using flowers instead of words to express nearly every emotion, from admiration to jealousy. Because flowers allowed people to reveal their feelings for one another in a subtle fashion, men and women could send and receive messages without fear of violating the proprieties of society.

Many dictionaries were published to help in deciphering the meanings of various flowers, but some couples undoubtedly invented their own flower language to ensure the secrecy of their floral communications.

Trillium
(Ardour)

Rose
(Love)

Giving meanings to the flowers they loved was one of the many ways in which Anne and her friends expressed their deep appreciation for the gifts of nature. As Anne helped Diana prepare for her wedding, she commented on Diana's choice of pink roses for her bridal bouquet ("After all, the only real roses are the pink ones…they are the flowers of love and faith"). Perhaps Anne chose roses for her own wedding bouquet because they symbolize love in all its forms – happy, hopeful, expectant, triumphant, joyous.

You can design your own meaningful bouquets to present to someone special. Use the meanings given here as a guide in composing your bouquets. You may want to use several different flowers in your bouquet, or you may want to do as Anne often did – use masses of one type of flower, such as pansies, for each bouquet. A few of the flower's leaves, tendrils of ivy or fern fronds added around the edges of the bouquet provide an accent for the flowers.

Little strips of paper with the meanings of the flowers written on them can be tucked among the flowers; an extra nice touch is to curl the papers by winding them around a pencil before you add them to the bouquet.

Tie the stems of the flowers together with ribbon, letting the ends of the ribbon trail down below the bouquet. You can also cut a small hole or "X" in the centre of a decorative paper doily and slip the stems into it so that the doily frames the bouquet with a lacy frill.

Bleeding Heart
(Yearning)

Anne's Garden
Through the Seasons

Spring

Spring was a special time for Anne, for it was the time when some of her favourite flowers made their appearance, from the first spring crocuses, daffodils, narcissi, tulips and lilies-of-the-valley to the late spring sweetpeas and nasturtiums.

Among Anne's very favourite garden flowers were pansies. There was a pansy bed at Green Gables, and "you found pansies everywhere at Ingleside." Pansies come in a wide variety of colours – gold, purple, white, yellow, blue, red – and their large petals have the sheen of velvet. They are annuals (plants that have to be started each year from seeds), but bloom from spring through summer. And, like most annuals, the more you pick them, the more they bloom!

Bleeding heart, columbine and peonies were among the perennial spring flowers (flowers that come up year after year) that surrounded Anne and Diana when they made their "solemn vow and promise" in the Barry garden at Orchard Slope. Peonies (or "pinies," as Mrs. Rachel Lynde called them) also grew in the gardens of Windy Poplars and Ingleside. Once they have been planted in a sunny location in rich soil, they will come up dependably year after year, providing huge, lusciously petalled flowers with a sweet rose-like scent. There are dozens of varieties of peonies – white, pink, red and mixed. Among Anne's favourites were "the milky-white peonies with the blood-red flecks at their hearts, like a god's kiss."

Lilacs were among the first things Anne noticed at Green Gables as she daydreamed at her window that first morning, when their

*Sweetpea
(Delight)*

*Pansy
(Thoughts)*

*Peony
(Shyness)*

"dizzily sweet fragrance drifted up to the window on the morning wind." Many years later, when Anne and Diana wandered together through the woods around Green Gables, Anne caught the scent of lilacs and asked, "Has it ever occurred to you, Diana, that there is something not quite…chaste…in the scent of lilac blossoms? …to me they always seem to be remembering some secret, *too*-sweet thing." Diana thought lilacs were "too heavy for the house," but we can think of few things nicer than a bowlful of purple lilacs in the spring.

Lilac
(First love)

In addition to the flowers she planted in her gardens, Anne loved to ramble through the woods and meadows around Avonlea, Kingsport, Summerside and Glen St. Mary to drink in the loveliness of all kinds of spring wildflowers. She and Diana found wild lilies-of-the-valley (they called them "June bells") on their way to school along the Birch Path, and Anne wore them "in the shining masses of her hair" when she was Diana's bridesmaid.

Anne felt sorry for people who lived where there were no Mayflowers, because to her, the "pink and white stars of sweetness" were "the souls of the flowers that died last summer." The schoolchildren of Avonlea went on Mayflower picnics, eating their lunch in a picturesque spot, playing games, gathering Mayflowers for bouquets and even making wreaths of them for their hats! Mayflowers continued to be Anne's special favourite ever after, and her son Jem "never forgot to take his mother a bouquet as long as they lasted." Mayflowers, also called trailing arbutus, are a protected species today, so they must not be picked or dug up. But if you manage to find some growing on a spring day, do sample their sweet fragrance and think of Anne.

Mayflower
(Thee only do I love)

Violets were another of Anne's spring delights. When she passed through the "big bowlful of violets" that was Violet Vale that first spring, her steps were reverent, "as if she trod on holy ground." Violets grow just about everywhere, preferring those shady glades that seem to enhance their qualities of shyness and modesty. Anne also looked for starflowers, trilliums and Adam-and-Eve.

Violet
(Faithfulness)

Two Garden Projects for the Spring

A Vaseful of Apple Blossoms

Before her first week at Green Gables had gone by, Anne had begun to transform Marilla's dinner table by bringing in a "jugful of apple blossoms" to decorate it. When a bee tumbled out of one of the blossoms, Anne was enchanted.

"Just think what a lovely place to live – in an apple blossom! Fancy going to sleep in it when the wind was rocking it. If I wasn't a human girl I think I'd like to be a bee and live among the flowers." (ANNE OF GREEN GABLES, VIII)

Just before spring, the buds of apple trees and other trees and shrubs begin to show on their branches. You can make them bloom early! Just cut a few apple, cherry or pussy willow branches (with permission, of course) and put them in a tall vase. Fill the vase with warm water and set it in a warm room. In a few days the buds will begin to swell, then bloom. Check the water level daily to make sure it doesn't get too low. It is also a good idea to pour out the old water every few days and put new water in.

*Apple Blossom
(Preference)*

*Geranium (scarlet)
(Comfort)*

A Little Plot to Call Your Own

If there is a little space in your yard to plant with flowers of your choice, there are many easy-to-grow flowers mentioned in the Anne books that you might want to consider. You can plant sweetpeas or bleeding heart for spring; nasturtiums, snapdragons or geraniums for summer; chrysanthemums for fall. Perhaps you would like to do as Anne did in her own little plot at Green Gables and include a few herbs or vegetables – lavender, mint, southernwood and caraway are herbs that Anne liked; she probably planted dill, sage and parsley, too. Carrots and lettuce have leaves that blend well with flowers, and they are easy to grow.

*Snapdragon
(Pride)*

If there is not a spot in the garden for you to call your own, try growing some ivy or honeysuckle entwined around a fencepost; or a pot of geraniums on a sunny corner of a porch or steps. Petunias are perfect for windowboxes – they will trail gracefully over the sides of the box and, especially in the evening, their fragrance will fill the air with sweetness.

SUMMER

Anne's favourite summer flowers were roses. She arrived at Green Gables in June, when the wild roses lining the lane to the house were just about to bloom; in fact, she noticed the very first rose of summer on that first morning, as she and Marilla were driving down the lane on their way to White Sands. Years later, when Marilla set a pot of miniature roses on Anne's windowsill to welcome her home from her year at Queen's, Anne called it "a song and a hope and a prayer all in one." She carried an armful of late-summer white roses at her wedding.

In addition to the lane's wild roses (*Rosa canina*), there were also the old white Scottish roses (*Rosa alba maxima*) that Matthew and Marilla's mother had brought with her from Scotland and planted at Green Gables. Since "Matthew always liked those roses the best – they were so small and sweet on their thorny stems," Anne took a slip from the Green Gables bush and planted it on his grave soon after he died.

The roses at Green Gables, Windy Poplars and the House of Dreams were the simple, hardy, old-fashioned varieties. They had been planted in the early 1800s, long before new varieties were developed later in that century. These old-fashioned roses had many uses. Anne and Diana used rose hips for making "necklaces of roseberries" the first summer Anne was at Green Gables. And Anne would have used rose hips (seed pods that develop after the

Petunia
(Modesty)

Fuchsia
(Taste)

Daisy
(Innocence)

flowers have bloomed) from the sweetbriar hedge that surrounded the Ingleside kitchen garden for making jam, jelly, tea and other treats. Rose petals are the main component of most old-fashioned potpourris (see page 87), and they can be candied and used as an elegant garnish for cakes and cookies.

Lilies of all kinds were also prized by Anne. The pure-white Madonna lilies grew in the Green Gables garden and "sent out whiffs of perfume that entered in on viewless winds at every door and window and wandered through halls and rooms like spirits of benediction" during the height of their June blooming. Anne and Diana became acquainted "gazing bashfully at one another over a clump of gorgeous tiger lilies" in the garden of Orchard Slope, and Anne planted the deep orange tiger lilies beside her front walk at Ingleside.

The easy-to-grow daylilies can be found in just about every garden on Prince Edward Island today! The flowers are trumpet-shaped like the Madonna lilies and tiger lilies, but the plants have long narrow leaves that form a fountain-like mound. The flower buds are borne on long stems that shoot up from the centre of each plant. Each flower blooms for only one day, but many buds per stem ensure that daylilies will bloom for several weeks in July and August. They were probably the "orange lilies at the gate of Anne's garden" at her House of Dreams.

No old-fashioned garden would really be complete without delphiniums, phlox and hollyhocks. Ingleside was well known for its delphiniums (also known as larkspur); one of Anne's friends made a special trip to see them one evening. And the Blythe children were measured by the Ingleside garden phlox, with its bright flower clusters blooming atop two- to three-foot plants all summer long. Hollyhocks, grown beside the front door at Green Gables and in front of the brick wall around Ingleside's garden, are officially biennial plants, which produce only leaves and a root system the first year; flowers and fruit or seeds the second. Hollyhocks have been favourite garden flowers in North America since the colonial days;

Phlox
(Our hearts are united)

Tiger Lily
(Gaiety)

Hollyhock
(Ambition)

in England since the 1400s. They produce many large red, white, pink or yellow flowers on their tall stalks; individual blossoms can be cut from the stem and floated in a shallow bowl of water for a striking effect.

Geraniums are very showy and come in many colours, from pure white to pink, salmon, red and even lavender. The leaves and flowers usually have a light spicy scent, but there are also varieties that have scents of mint, lemon, orange, nutmeg or apple. Marilla had an apple-scented geranium on the kitchen windowsill at Green Gables; Anne named it Bonny the first morning she was there. Geraniums were popular houseplants at that time because they were said to keep away flies. The leaves of scented geraniums can be used as flavourings in custards, cakes and jellies; the dried scented leaves and petals can be added to potpourri.

Geranium (apple-scented)
(Meeting)

Marigold
(Affection)

Bouncing Bet
(Flawless)

Cheerful marigolds, too, bloom all summer and into the fall. They grew in the gardens of Patty's Place and the House of Dreams. They come in shades of gold, from lightest lemon to deep orange with touches of rust, and they do well in pots, windowboxes and garden plots. Kitchen gardens are often surrounded by a border of marigolds, because they help keep insects away from the fruits and vegetables. However, they can grow as tall as three feet, so the dwarf varieties (about 12 inches high) are usually best for edging beds or for growing in pots. Marigolds have a nice spicy fragrance, so dry blooms go well in potpourri bowls.

Some unusual summer perennials grew in the Barry garden at Orchard Slope. The "lilac-tinted Bouncing Bets" (also known as latherwort, soapwort, bruisewort, Fuller's herb, lady's washbowl and old-maid's pink) grow one to two feet high. The flowers are about one inch across and grow in clusters at the tops of the stems; they have a spicy fragrance. Now found growing wild in many areas of North America, Bouncing Bet was brought from England by early colonists for use as a cleaning agent – when its roots and leaves are boiled in water, the resulting concoction is a very gentle but effective detergent!

Poppy
(Consolation)

Bluebell
(Constancy)

Alyssum
(Worth beyond beauty)

The "scarlet lightning that shot its fiery lances over prim white musk-flowers" in the Barry garden is another name for Maltese cross or Jerusalem cross. Its bright-red flowers grow in clusters; the plant grows to about three feet high. Musk-flowers are also known as musk roses or musk mallows; they grow to about two feet. Both bloom in July and August.

Other summer perennials that Anne had in her gardens were dahlias, iris and Oriental poppies (which were used to decorate Green Gables' parlour grate in Mrs. Morgan's honour).

The "golden frenzy of wind-stirred buttercups" that inspired Anne's scandalous hat adornment were probably the wild buttercups that grow freely nearly everywhere on Prince Edward Island from May to September.

Other summer wildflowers Anne loved were daisies, Shirley poppies, "ladies' eardrops" (wild fuchsia), bluebells, honeysuckle and the water lilies that grew on the Lake of Shining Waters.

A Garden Project for the Summer

A Nosegay in a Flowerpot

A nosegay (small bunch of flowers) grown in a flowerpot will last much longer than one made from cut flowers. Try a potted bouquet of pansies and sweet alyssum (sometimes called "carpet of snow" or "snowdrift" because of the tiny white flowers, hardly bigger than a snowflake, that cover these low-growing plants); or, instead of pansies you could use dwarf marigolds or petunias.

You will need a large flowerpot, at least 12 inches across; enough small rocks or pebbles (1 inch or less in diameter) to cover the bottom of the pot about 1 inch deep; potting soil; a trowel; three or four pansy plants and six to eight sweet alyssum plants (available at nursery or garden stores).

Chrysanthemum (white)
(Truth)

1 Put the pebbles in the bottom of the pot to help hold the soil in and to provide good drainage for the plants' roots.

2 Fill the pot with potting soil, to within about 2 inches of the rim.

3 Pour enough water into the soil to moisten it throughout – about 2 to 3 cups. Stir the soil.

Rice Lily
(Rarity)

4 Remove the pansy plants from their nursery pots and plant them a few inches apart in the middle of the flowerpot. Push the potting soil aside to make a space for each plant, put the plant into the space and gently press the soil around it to hold it in place.

5 Remove the alyssum plants from their nursery pots and plant them about 4 inches apart around the inner edge of the pot. This will look like a little lacy frill around the pansies.

6 Water each plant well. Put the pot outside in a bright sunny spot. Water the plants every other day, or whenever the top surface of the soil feels dry. Pick off the pansy flowers as they begin to wither. This will encourage the plants to grow more flowers and will keep them from sprawling too far over the pot.

Scarlet Lightning
(Radiance)

FALL

Chrysanthemum (gold)
(Slighted love)

Goldenrod
(Encouragement)

Aster
(Variety)

Chrysanthemums are the glory of fall. Not only are they at their best then, but they last long after most of the summer flowers. Some chrysanthemums are even hardy enough to survive winter planted in the garden. Shades of "gold and russet," such as were found in the spruce corner of Ingleside's lawn, are the most popular, but there are also white chrysanthemums. The size and shape of the flowers can vary widely, from simple daisy-like blossoms to the huge pom-poms popular as football-game corsages.

While chrysanthemums are the glory of the fall garden, goldenrod is the glory of North American fields and roadsides in the fall. There are many species of goldenrod, but what other than the Canadian goldenrod could be Anne's? It blooms from July through September and can grow to six feet tall! Anise-flavoured goldenrod leaves were used in place of tea leaves in Colonial America after the Boston Tea Party, and Indians used goldenrod tea as an ointment for wounds. Goldenrod flowers can also be used to make dye and can be easily dried for use in arrangements. (Incidentally, contrary to popular belief, goldenrod pollen is *not* the cause of common hayfever; ragweed, which blooms during the same period but much more subtly, must bear the blame for that nuisance!)

Anne also loved the "dainty little wild orchids which Avonlea children called 'rice lilies'" (more commonly known as ladies' tresses), the tiny daisy-like wild blue asters that grew in Rainbow Valley behind Ingleside, and pigeonberries, also known as partridgeberries. Pigeonberry vines bloom with tiny white flowers in the spring, but it was the "scarlet tufts" of fall berries that Anne loved. The berries are long-lasting; you can still find them in winter on their low-growing evergreen vines. A traditional decoration at Christmas is a "partridgeberry bowl" – the cuttings of shiny green leaves and bright-red berries can be rooted in peat moss, kept moist, and planted in spring as a ground cover after their holiday usefulness is past. They thrive in woodsy settings, even under evergreens.

Two Garden Projects for the Fall

*Daffodil
(Admiration;
unrequited love)*

A Spring Bulb Garden

Fall is the time to plant bulbs for the following spring's first flowers. All you need are bulbs from your local nursery, a trowel and a spot in your garden. If you don't have much space, try a tiny clump of daffodils by your doorstep or under a tree; in the spring, the golden trumpets will lift your spirits after a long winter.

Daffodils look their best when planted in groups or clumps, not lined up in stiff rows. One way to achieve this effect, called "naturalizing," is to gently toss a handful in the area you want to plant them and dig the hole for each bulb where it lands. Plant each bulb about 6 to 8 inches deep, with the bulbs no less than 2 inches apart. Place the bulb (flat side down) in the hole and then cover it with soil.

In addition to daffodils, you can plant narcissi, the smaller-cupped, fragrant flowers that Anne and Diana called "June lilies." When they come up in the spring, you might even be able to imagine yourself in Hester Gray's garden, where hundreds of yellow and white narcissi had spread through the years to make the hidden spot look as if it "were carpeted with moonshine and sunshine combined." Or you can try planting tulips; Anne and little Jem planted red, gold and purple ones one "gold-grey smoky afternoon" at Ingleside, knowing that they would spend the winter underground in preparation for their spectacular display of colour the following spring. We should warn you that squirrels find tulip bulbs a very tasty treat and are likely to dig them up almost as soon as you have planted them. Some people plant their tulips in little "baskets" they make from wire mesh to prevent squirrel damage, but if there are lots of squirrels near your hoped-for tulip bed, you might want to plant more daffodils and narcissi instead.

*Southernwood
(Jest)*

*Tulip
(Fame; love)*

In the spring, after your bulbs have finished blooming, cut the flower stems off and discard them, but don't cut the leaves. The bulbs will take nourishment from them for multiplying and to produce the next season's blooms, so you must wait patiently for the leaves to turn brown and dry before you cut them off. Try loosely braiding the leaves of each plant and curling them over while they are drying, to make them look a little more attractive. You can also plant some annuals around the bulbs to help hide the drying foliage.

A Tabletop Garden

You can even have an Anne garden on a tabletop! It's so easy and will delight you in every season.

You will need a large basket, about 16 inches across and 5 inches deep; a metal or plastic dish to fit inside the basket to make the basket waterproof; five plants in 4-inch pots – different kinds of ivy, ferns and other houseplants are good; Spanish moss (florists and nurseries sell bags of this curly grey moss).

Lily (white)
(Purity; sweetness)

Ivy
(Friendship; marriage)

Nasturtium
(Selfishness)

1 Line the bottom of the basket with the metal or plastic dish.

2 Set the plants in the basket with one plant in the centre and the others around the edge.

3 Water the plants, making sure the liner catches any drips.

4 Tuck Spanish moss around the pots to hide the edges and fill in any spaces between the pots.

5 Set your tabletop garden in the spot you have selected for it – in the centre of the dining table or on a coffee table, perhaps.

6 Water the plants about once a week.

Honeysuckle
(Generous affection;
devoted love)

One of our favourite tabletop gardens changes slightly with the seasons. While the green plants around the edges of the basket remain constant, the centre plant is replaced every few months with different seasonal flowering plants – a small pot of daffodils or tulips in spring; geraniums in summer; chrysanthemums in fall; and a miniature evergreen tree in winter, decorated with tiny red velvet bows!

Fern
(Sincerity; fascination)

A desktop or dressing-table garden could be put together along the same lines as the tabletop garden, using a smaller basket and 2-inch potted plants. A few small silk or dried flowers tucked in here and there would add a nice touch. This would also make a delightful gift.

Buttercup
(Riches; memories
of childhood)

WINTER

Not much gardening goes on in winter for, as Anne said to Marilla one cold November evening, "All the little wood things – the ferns and the satin leaves and the crackerberries – have gone to sleep, just as if somebody had tucked them away until spring under a blanket of leaves."

You can, however, squeeze a little bit of early spring out of the cold wintertime.

A Garden Project for the Winter

A Winter-Spring Garden

Besides Mayflowers, Anne's favourite spring flowers were narcissi. But Anne could easily have had narcissi in the middle of winter! This is what she would have had to do; you can try it yourself.

You will need a waterproof bowl or pot, about 8 inches across and several inches deep; enough pebbles or gravel to fill the bowl about halfway up; five "paperwhite" narcissi bulbs. (You can buy special bulbs that are designed for forcing, or buy regular narcissi bulbs and put them in the refrigerator or other cold-but-not-freezing spot for about six weeks before you plant them.)

Start the bulbs about four weeks before you want the flowers to bloom. Some people like to start their paperwhites around the first of December so that they will bloom in time for Christmas. (Anne liked narcissi so much, she might have started another pot of bulbs two weeks after the first one so she would have them around twice as long.) When your narcissi bloom, use them as a table centrepiece at your Anne tea party (see Chapter 5), and impress your friends with your green thumb!

Pigeonberry
(Indifference)

Narcissus
(Selfishness)

Lavender
(Hesitation)

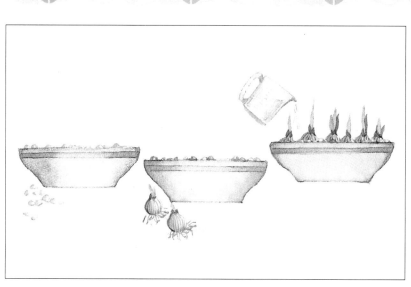

Muskflower
(Charm)

1 Place the pebbles in the bowl.

2 Scoop out a little space in the pebbles to set each bulb in, flat side down. The pebbles should come up about halfway around the bulb to hold it upright.

3 When the bulbs are in place, pour enough water in to come up to the base of the bulbs. Keep the water level at the base of the bulbs. At first, the bulbs may need to be watered every day or so, because they grow quickly!

4 Soon you will notice buds forming at the ends of the flower stems. Then the buds will bloom and you will have sweet little white clusters of blossoms that are very fragrant. You may want to tie a ribbon around the plants as they get taller to keep them upright.

Right after Christmas, nursery catalogues begin to appear with their tempting offerings for spring planting. You can spend the next few months poring over them as Anne loved to do, planning what you will fill your garden or windowboxes or planters with after the last frost of the season.

Waterlily
(Purity of heart; eloquence)

Cherry Blossom
(Education)

IN CONCLUSION

Anne began life impoverished and unloved, yet she managed to cultivate her gifts of optimism, curiosity and imagination. As a girl she was impetuous and adventurous, but she developed into a young woman of courage and independence, as her romantic notions mellowed into an intense appreciation for beauty and accomplishment.

Though Anne was of a much different era, we can still share those things she valued most – "the joys of sincere work and worthy aspiration and congenial friendship." And perhaps we can be counted among her cherished kindred spirits, for she once said herself that "kindred spirits are not so scarce as I used to think. It's splendid to find out there are so many of them in the world."

DESIGN, ART DIRECTION AND TYPOGRAPHY: Pronk&Associates

ILLUSTRATION: David Bathurst 30, 32 – 43
   Bernadette Lau 56, 58 – 64, 67 – 69, 71 – 76, 78, 80, 82
   Barbara Massey cover, ii, vii, x, xii, xiii, 17(silhouettes), 18, 19, 31, 44,
      45, 54, 55, 84, 110, 111, 113, 115, 117, 119, 121, 122, 123, 142
   Jack McMaster 7, 14 – 15, 20, 22
   Carol Paton 3, 17(tree), 85, 124 – 141, 143
   Margo Stahl 28 – 29, 86, 88 – 93, 95 – 107, Line art: 113, 115, 117, 119, 121

PHOTOGRAPHY: Ian Crysler 8 – 13

E. Stuart Macdonald Estate and L. M. Montgomery Collection, Archival Collection, University of Guelph Library: 2

Osborne Collection of Early Children's Books, Toronto Public Library: Book covers 8, 9, 10, 11(top), 12(top), 13

Public Archives of Prince Edward Island: 49, 50

We are grateful to McClelland & Stewart Inc. for allowing us to photograph the covers of *Anne of Windy Poplars* and *Anne of Ingleside* which appear on pages 11 and 12. *Anne of Windy Poplars* by L. M. Montgomery was originally published by McClelland & Stewart, Limited. Copyright, Canada, 1936 by McClelland & Stewart, Limited. *Anne of Ingleside* was originally published by McClelland & Stewart, Limited. Copyright, Canada, 1939 by McClelland & Stewart, Limited.